W9-CCD-478

Anointed Inspirations Publishing

Presents

Mama Raised Me
but
Her Demons Changed Me

A novel by

Denora M. Boone

Note: This is a work of fiction. Names, characters, places and incidents either are products of the author's imagination or are used fictitiously. Any resemblance to actual events or locales or persons, living or dead, is entirely coincidental

Anointed Inspirations Publishing is currently accepting Urban Christian Fiction, Inspirational Romance, and Young Adult fiction submissions. For consideration please send manuscripts to Anointedinspirationspublishing@gmail.com

Connect with Denora socially
Facebook: www.facebook.com/AuthorDenora
Twitter: www.twitter.com/mzboone27
Instagram: @mzboone81
www.authordenora.com

God.

My Husband Byron.

Our children (Jalen, Elijah, Mekiyah, and Isaiah).

#AIP.

My readers.

These are the ones I do this for and the ones who won't allow me to quit. For that, all of my thanks go to them!

Love,

Dee

Prologue

"Oh my God it's now or never," I thought as I watched Amir getting undressed.

I had been with plenty men before now but just like always I was shaking like a leaf. Pulling the covers up under my neck I tried thinking of a way out of this but I knew that it was too late. I had fallen for Amir, or at least I thought I had, years ago and although he was in a relationship with someone else I didn't care. It was as if my soul craved him to survive.

"What's good? You changing your mind on me?" Amir asked me.

"No. It's just that this is my first time and I'm a little nervous," I lied through my teeth.

"Don't even trip. I'll take my time I promise."

Deciding not to say anything I just smiled at him as he moved closer to where I sat. The moment his knee hit the bed and he went to pull the covers back we heard the front door open.

"KiKi!" I heard my mother yell.

"Shoot!" Amir said in a panic while I sat frozen in place.

This couldn't be happening. Not now. My mama was supposed to be out of town for the weekend at a church retreat and here I was sneaking around with her boyfriend.

"You just gonna sit there?" Amir asked as he fumbled around with his pants. Before he could get his left leg inside of his jeans my door burst open and there stood my mother.

"What is going on here?" My mama asked as soon as the bedroom door swung open. Stopping dead in her tracks she just stood there with her mouth wide open in shock and tears forming in her eyes.

As bad as I wanted to roll my eyes at my mother I didn't. Did I want her to find out like this? Did I want her to hurt like I was hurting? Of course. I just wanted to succeed in my plan first before I ended her world.

"Baby it's not what you think," Amir did his best to explain reaching for her.

"Oh, it's exactly what I'm thinking! You're about to sleep with my son!" She yelled and I dropped my head.

"Son?!"

"Yes, my son Kiondre," my mama shrieked before she snatched my wig off.

If looks could kill I would be dead. And if the looks from both my mother and Amir didn't kill me I was sure that the bullets from the gun he was now holding would do the job.

"What's the long face for?" my cellmate asked causing me to come back to the present.

"Man bruh just thinking," I told him.

"Well I know if it was me I would be showing all thirty-two of my teeth round here. Ain't no better feeling than being let out. What? You not happy?"

"It's just hard to believe his day is finally here that's all," I lied.

Instead of telling him my real thoughts, I busied myself around the small cell gathering the little bit of items that I had accumulated over the last twenty years. It wasn't much but they did hold sentimental value for me. Letters from my grandmother, a few books, and my Bible.

See, I had been serving time for the murder of my mother's boyfriend Amir for the last fifteen years but today was my release day. No matter how hard I tried to get those thoughts out of my head they were still as vivid as the day that it had happened. I just prayed that once I was out in society again that everyday life would help me to forget. Being stuck up in this hell hole only reminded me daily of the life I took. There were plenty of times that I wanted to just end my own life so the torment would subside. But I couldn't bring myself to do so.

"Andrews! Let's get it," one of the guards said as he opened the cell door.

"Aight then bruh you stay up!" my cellmate dapped me up excitedly.

I grabbed my things and as I walked down the corridor said farewell to a few of the other inmates before going through the doors to process out. In less than twenty I would be a free man but I didn't know how I felt about that. Being that when I was arrested I was only fifteen years old, I didn't know how to survive on my own. Survival in jail was different than survival in the streets. At least in here I had a roof over my head, clothes, and three meals a day. The basics. I was about to walk out into society with nothing but a GED and two thousand dollars that was saved from working around the jail. My grandmother Myrtle made sure to keep my books full even on a fixed income so I made sure to save my other money so that I could help her out even just a little bit until I got on my feet.

After I was done being processed I was a free man. The realization of that hit me as soon as I heard the security doors to St. Clair Correctional Facility close behind me and I stepped out into the bright sunlight. Closing my eyes, I took a deep breath of the fresh air as the tears ran down my face. I was so overwhelmed that I didn't care if anyone saw me crying. If they had never experienced the things that I had in the thirty years I had been on this earth then they wouldn't understand. As I walked to the awaiting shuttle that took released inmates to the nearest Greyhound bus station, I couldn't help but to think of what lied ahead of me once I touched back down in my hometown of Macon, Georgia.

Tayler

I knew I should have turned my phone off the moment I clocked out of work. I had just completed my third straight sixteen-hour shift on only four hours of sleep and I was beyond tired. The only reason that I hadn't cut myself completely off from the world was because of my fifteen-year-old daughter, my mother, and my uncle. Although Justice stayed with them on the nights that I had to work, she was also there to watch them just in case something happened to either of them and I wasn't able to get to them in time. It wasn't that they had Alzheimer's or anything, they just liked to fight. Not in a physical way but verbally. My mother Agnes was a petty queen. She would say whatever she wanted to my uncle Clifford if he pushed her buttons enough and when she went in, I mean she went all the way in.

Looking down at my phone I saw my mother's number flash across the screen and before I could answer it stopped ringing only to start back up. This time Justice's picture popped up. That only meant one thing, old Agnes and OG Cliff Daddy as he liked to be called, were at it again.

"Lord give me the strength," I said right before I picked up the phone. "Hey Jussie."

"Ma," Justice began but couldn't hold her laughter in. She loved when her grandmother went off and swore that it was the funniest thing that she had ever heard. That was one of the reasons that she never minded going over there. As tired as I was right now I couldn't help but to join in and wait to hear the latest shenanigans.

Growing up I was just like Justice and couldn't wait until Momma got to popping off at the mouth. Even my friends wanted to be around when our house got live. Agnes loved the Lord and stayed in church but would go off at the drop of a dime. She may not have cussed but her clapbacks were so full of fire that you would think she had.

As I waited for my poor child to gather herself, I threw my thick comforter back and stood up to get dressed. My body was screaming for some sleep but if I didn't go and play referee then I knew sleep would be even further away. The quicker I could get them under control the faster I could visit my boo, Mr. Sandman.

Grabbing a pair of sweats from my drawer I threw them over my shapely legs before grabbing a hoodie and slipping my feet into my slides. My freshly pressed hair was all over my head as I looked at my cinnamon colored face in the mirror. Being that I worked in a factory, I moved around all day and that helped me to stay a solid size 18. I was on the tall side so the weight was well proportioned and I got no complaints.

"Girrrllllllll," Justice screeched causing me to have to pull the phone away from my ear momentarily.

"Uh no ma'am! What did I tell you about talking to me like I'm one of your little friends Justice?" I asked her once I replaced the phone. I was close to my daughter and we had a very good relationship but she knew that I wasn't her friend. I was her mother and she was taught to respect me as that.

"No mommy I wasn't talking to you. Cadence is here with me," she informed me.

"Hey Momma Tay!" I heard her best friend yell from the background before falling into a fit of uncontrollable laughter.

My phone was housed in a case that doubled as a wallet so all I had to do was grab my keys and head out. Making sure everything was off in the house I locked up and walked over to my car. Just as I was about to speak I heard what sounded like a slap in the background before hearing my uncle cry out in pain.

"Nana no!" I heard Justice say before giggling.

"What happened?" I asked as I put on my seatbelt and started the car. It would only take me about ten minutes to get to the other side of Decatur but the way I was feeling I knew that it was going to feel like ten hours.

Instead of Justice responding I heard Cadence tell me to hurry up because Nana was "turnt", whatever that meant. I couldn't keep up with teens these days and their lingo. I let her know that I was on my way and to try and help keep things as calm as possible. We didn't need the police called again although I think they liked getting the calls. It was entertaining to say the least and made for good stories down at the jail.

Almost fifteen minutes later I pulled up to the house and prayed that I could get them loving each other again in less than five. My eyes were barely open and if I didn't know any better I swear that I had fallen asleep behind the wheel. To God be the glory I made it safe and unharmed. The moment I got out of the car I could hear my mama going at it and the girls laughing. I mentally prepared myself for what I was about to face. The way the two of them constantly argued one would think they were married instead of siblings but as far back as I could remember they had always been like this. Make no mistake about it though they loved each other unconditionally but didn't like the other one bit. I'm still not sure why they even lived together but I guess it was because they really didn't want to be alone at their age.

My parents had me late in life. They were 45 years old when I was born and their only child. Harper, the world's best father, passed when I was nine and it broke both me and my momma's hearts. Not long after that my uncle Clifford moved in because he said that we needed to be protected and he had been there ever since.

"I bet if you bring Gertrude ole moonshine drinking, kitten heel wearing, dusty wig having self over here again it's gone be a situation. I done told you I don't like the wanch!" I heard my mother yell followed by Justice and Cadence's laughs.

The moment I opened the door I almost peed on myself from laughing at the sight before me. Poor Agnes must have been in the middle of watching her stories because she had on her "round the house coat" with the pink flowers and her sponge rollers in her hair. The rollers wouldn't have been so out of place if they weren't attached to her wig. I never understood why she didn't just take it off to curl it and why she had to walk around with it on her head like it was real. She had one of her old worn out slippers that I swear she had since I was a child in one hand and the other one on her foot. She was just about to haul off and it him if Justice hadn't stepped in front of her.

"Wanch?! Call my lady a wanch again and see what happens," Uncle Clifford said.

"How 'bout you try and see period you old fool! Glasses thick like a bottle and you still can't see how to dress. Looking like you put on your clothes in the dark while still inside the closet," Momma fired back.

I couldn't help the tears falling from my eyes as I observed his attire. She was right, he did look like he had no clue about what he was putting on. Uncle Clifford was a round old man who put you in the mind of Redd Foxx. His grey hair was only around the sides of his head resembling a cul-de-sac with the middle of his head just as bald as a baby's bottom. Patches of hair was missing in his beard but you couldn't tell him or Ms. Gertrude that he wasn't the finest thing in Decatur.

What got me though was his outfit of choice. He had on a pair of slightly high-water doo doo brown slacks that looked to be made of wool, his white wife beater was three sizes too small and rose just above his protruding belly. He wore a soft pink button up that only had a few buttons secure but they were buttoned incorrectly, causing the shirt to be in a zig zag pattern. And on his feet, Jesus his feet. This man had on a pair of sandals that looked like he was about to cook some mean barbecue but his feet were ashy and they rolled over to the outside. He looked a hot mess but I loved my uncle and so did his boo Gertrude.

"Momma what's going on?" I was finally able to get out. I was so out of breath from laughing and wiping my tears that it took me a minute to be able to speak.

"When did you get here?" she asked me instead of answering my question.

"Heyyyy there go my pretty thang!" Uncle Clifford said excitedly with not one tooth in his mouth. For as long as I could remember that had been his nickname for me.

"Don't try to get my child on your side!"

Before he could respond Justice jumped in to explain what was going on while I did my best to stay as alert as I could. Sleep was calling me and I wanted to answer so bad.

"Nana caught Ms. Gertrude coming out of Uncle Clif-," she started before he cut her off.

"OG Cliff Daddy!" he corrected her sternly and it took everything in me to not die from laughing.

"OG must stand for Old Goat," my momma said rolling her eyes at him.

"Anyway, Nana caught Ms. Gertrude trying to sneak out when Guiding Light went to commercial and they got into it." Justice explained.

"I told her she had to move fast but OG put it on her and had her moving slow," he grinned.

"Ewwww," everyone else said in unison. That was a visual that I could do without.

"How you expect her to move fast with that peg leg? Round here looking like a pirate with no ship."

"Ohhh Momma that was wrong," I told her but on the inside I was a weak mess.

"What? It's true and you know it. He thought that because I was into my stories that I wouldn't know what was going on and when I got up right quick to get some water here she come hobbling out the room."

"Keep on Agnes and watch me kick you in your bad hip," he yelled at her. What did he say that for?

"Do it then since you bad!" she yelled back.

"Come on now y'all that's enough. Uncle Clifford-."

"*O-G Cliff Daddy!*"

"OG Cliff Daddy, you know the history between Momma and Ms. Gertrude so why would you bring her here?" I asked.

"Because I hid the car keys from him. Trying to get out there and drive knowing his license been revoked since '73. What I'm gonna do if he gets out there and kills someone or himself?" she asked sincerely. And just like that her whole mood had changed.

"See Unc, I mean OG, she was just looking out for you by taking the keys. It really didn't have much to do with Ms. Gertrude," I let him know.

"Yes it did too," she mumbled just loud enough for me to hear.

"Well I didn't think about it like that I guess," he replied.

This was the part where they made up like they always did for a few hours but would be right back at it later.

"You know I love you, you old goat," she told him before dropping her slipper and sitting back down in her rocker.

"I love you too even if we have the same haircut under that wig of yours."

"Uncle Clifford!"

"What I do?" he asked before heading back down the hall to his room.

"Babyyy I love coming over here," Cadence laughed and Justice agreed before they both walked outside on the porch.

"Tay-ter Pie you look so sleepy. Gone in that room back there and lay down and after I finish my stories that I missed I will make dinner for us all."

Not having enough energy to refuse her offer I gladly accepted and headed to my old room. All I needed was a few hours of sleep and I would be able to function. I just prayed that my mother and uncle behaved themselves long enough for me to rest.

Tayler

Lord knows I needed that sleep. I could use a little more but that could wait until I got back home to my bed. The smell of fried chicken, fresh collard greens with the smoked ham hock, baked macaroni and cheese, and cornbread assaulted my nose alerting my stomach that it was time to get down. I don't even remember the last time I ate because I had been so busy working and my stomach was letting me know it wasn't for the shenanigans today.

Stretching long and hard I felt and heard my bones pop but it felt so good. I stood up and noticed that the sun was shining bright and that was odd. When I had laid down it was well into the day so it should have been dark by now. I pulled back the lavender curtain to see the street that my mama lived on was full of people coming up and down the street.

"Ma!" I yelled looking for my phone that I couldn't find.

"What you doing all that hollin' foe guh?" she opened the door fussing.

"I can't find my phone. What time is it?" I asked as I moved the covers on the bed and checked under the pillows. I knew that it was beside me when I laid down.

"I took it 'cause it was ringing off the hook last night and I didn't want it to disturb you. I know you needed your rest," she told me.

"Last night?"

"Chile it's almost three in the afternoon. A few times I had to come and put my finger under your nose to make sure you were still breathing. Why you workin' yourself so hard baby?" she asked with a face full of concern.

This was one conversation that I wasn't trying to have right then. As long as my daughter was taken care of and I was able to put a significant amount of money into savings I was good.

"Not now ma," I said before rubbing my temples.

Putting her hands up in mock surrender she pursed her lips together. I knew that look too well and she was not about to let it go all the way.

"All I'm saying baby is that there is still life after divorce. That one man couldn't break you so live a little while you still have time. Maybe give me another grandbaby," she laughed.

"Baby?!" Justice screeched only hearing the end of the conversation. "Mommy you pregnant?" she wanted to know. Her big beautiful eyes wide with excitement.

"You been sneaking into your uncle's liquor cabinet Jus 'cause you must be drunk?" I asked her seriously.

Uncle Cliff drank that backwoods moonshine and loved to keep a stash in the back of his closet. I knew it was back there because he had been hiding it in the same place since I was a teen. Me and my best friend Nola would always sneak in there and get a little taste on occasion when we wanted to be grown. He would always wonder why he was short but we would convince him that he had been the one to drink it. He fell for it every time and went right back to Mr. Johnny for some more.

Sucking her teeth in disappointment, Justice walked out of the room followed by my mama and then myself. Shaking my head, I stopped at the linen closet and retrieved a face cloth from the shelf before heading back into my old bathroom to wash my face and brush my teeth. I would shower once I ate and throw on something that I was sure I had in the closet.

Once I was done I made my way to the kitchen to see Mama making plates for everyone so I grabbed the cups from the cabinet and began pouring our drinks. Once we were done we all sat down together to say grace and dig in.

"Mommy you feeling alright? You don't ever sleep so long," Justice asked me. That little girl acted like she was my mama sometimes but I loved that about her. She was so mature for her age but still carried herself like the child she was.

"Yes baby I'm fine. Those hours working finally just caught up with me. If anyone calls out I have to fill in." I said praying that she believed me. I hated lying to my child but some things I kept from her because it wasn't her burden to carry.

I didn't think she needed to know I worked so much because it kept my mind off of her father who had walked out on us just four years ago. I never wanted my baby to feel like I was avoiding her but if I was going to be honest with myself, some days I was. Just looking at Justice with her smooth chocolate skin, big brown almond shaped eyes, long curly hair, and one dimple in her right cheek would remind me of her father. She was the spitting image of Corey and took it so hard when he left us.

I would never forget the day that I came in from work early. The shift that I was supposed to be working was an overnight one and I wasn't scheduled to get off until 7am the next morning. At the time I was three months pregnant with our second child and hadn't been feeling good since clocking in that evening. By midnight I couldn't take it anymore. My feet were swollen and the bottom of my stomach was cramping. I wasn't spotting or anything thankfully, so I just figured I needed a good night's rest.

Once my supervisor looked at me, she demanded that I go home and take a few days off. The drive home felt like it took forever causing me to take a sigh of relief the moment I parked in our driveway. Getting out I saw that Corey's car was parked which surprised me. He was a lawyer and when we had spoken a few hours before he had told me that he would be in the office all night. Justice was with my mother since neither of us was home. For him to not tell me that he had gotten off early was odd but I didn't care. I just wanted to shower and lay my head on his chest.

The minute I unlocked the side door that we always used I knew something was off. There were two glasses sitting on our bar and from where I stood one of them looked as if it had lipstick around the rim. I knew for a fact that it wasn't my glass or shade. Making my way through the kitchen I sat my purse on the counter but not before grabbing the Ruger 380 with the purple handle that Corey had gotten me one year on my birthday. The only time that I had ever pulled the trigger was at the range but I had a feeling that if what I saw didn't line up with the will of God it was about to be on.

Instead of heading towards the soft light that was glowing under the closed door of the den, I decided to check out the rest of the house first just to make sure. Or maybe I was just praying that if I waited to open the door I wouldn't walk in on something that was sure to cause my house to be on the next episode of *The First 48*. Each room I checked there was nothing that was out of the norm so I headed back downstairs and stood frozen outside of the den.

"I know good and well..." I whispered to myself before leaning my head closer to the door just to get confirmation.

"Are you sure she won't be home anytime soon?" the female asked. It was a familiar one. Too familiar.

"I already told you Tay is working overnight. Now come show daddy how much you missed me," I heard my so-called husband say.

It took everything in me not to release the dinner that I had eaten earlier before I placed my hand on the knob and took the safety off. Taking a deep breath, I opened the door slowly and was faced with my worst fear. Sitting on the large sectional that was the location of many family movie nights and spur of the moment love making sessions between my husband and I, was the man that I married. He definitely wasn't alone as I watched the light skin thick woman with hair reaching her middle back begin to lower her body on to his.

"Ssssss, Kay," he hissed once contact was made.

As bad as I wanted to raise my gun and get these fireworks started like the Fourth of July I was stuck. I could feel the anger rising from the bottom of my feet and traveling its way up my body. I was on fire from the inside out but couldn't move. That was until a pain in my lower stomach and back almost crippled me.

"Mmph!" I mumbled lowly but not low enough.

"Oh shoot! Tayler its not what you think," the woman said jumping her naked body up and scrambling to get to her clothes that were strewn about.

"It's exactly what I think First Lady and I'm sure that Pastor would think so too if he was here."

That's right my husband and the woman who was supposed to be our spiritual leader were having an affair.

"Let's just talk about this baby. I'm sure we can work this out," Corey pleaded with wide eyes. He was talking to me but his focus was on the shaky hand that was holding the object that was about to take him to the King. Obviously, he was ready to gone on to glory.

Before I could even respond to what he said or the fact that Kay was just standing there, the warm wet sensation I felt between my legs all of a sudden caused me to look down and see the light blue scrubs that I was wearing turning red.

Dropping the gun on the floor, I used both of my hands to grab the bottom of my stomach while sliding down the door frame.

"Tayler!" Corey yelled out running over to me. As bad as I didn't want him touching me the pain took control of my body and all I wanted him to do was get me some help.

I knew that I should have just been seen at the hospital but I didn't think it was that serious. My mind made me think that I was just tired and a little rest would do the trick but now I understood it was something more.

Corey didn't even bother saying anything to Kay before he pushed her out of the door and ran back to pick me up. Placing me in the backseat of his truck he hopped into the driver's seat and sped out of our neighborhood. The whole way to the hospital all he kept doing was apologizing for what he as I cried my eyes out. The tears that fell down my face weren't only for the baby that I knew was no more but for the end of my marriage.

"It hurts," I moaned in pain as I rocked back and forth.

"I know baby we are almost there. Just hold on Tay. Oh God I'm sorry. Please keep my wife safe."

His voice was becoming muffled and I could feel myself losing consciousness as I fought to stay awake. My eyes were getting heavy and I felt like I was sitting in a freezer naked I was so cold. I was losing so much blood and I knew it.

"Tayler! Tayler! Can you hear me?" I heard one of the nurses yelling but it was so faint. I wanted to speak but I couldn't and the last thing that I remembered before my eyes closed completely was Kay along with her husband and our pastor standing beside Corey.

"Earth to Tay," my mama called out and snapping her fingers in my face to get my attention. Once again, the memory of my past had taken over making me feel like I was in that moment again.

I looked around the table and just like always everyone was looking at me with sympathy in their eyes. I hated that and wished they wouldn't do that. Especially Justice. The pain etched on her face made me feel like less of a mother because I couldn't take her hurt away. I would gladly take hers away and add it to mine if I could. It took her quite some time to get through what her father did, the divorce, and losing a sibling at such a young age but she was definitely strong.

"Sorry ma. What did you say?" I asked.

"Myrtle just called and asked if you could do her a favor."

"What's that?"

"Her grandson was on his way here but his last bus was late causing him to miss the one from Atlanta to Macon. Do you think you can go get him for her? I'll give you the gas money."

"Mama stop it. You know I'm not taking your money. Let her know I don't mind. Just let me go shower and change real quick," I told her getting up from the table.

It took me less than thirty minutes to get ready in some ripped jeans, an Atlanta Falcon's t-shirt, and my black Fenty Puma slides. When I got to the front room my mama stopped me before going into the kitchen and coming back with a thermal lunch bag and a soda.

"I'll eat when I get back Mama," I told her looking down at the bag. There was no way that I could eat like I wanted to while driving. Not only that, but I knew that once I did finish that plate it would be time to knock out once again.

"It's not for you baby. It's for Myrtle's grandson Kiondre. He hasn't had a homecooked meal in quite some time now so I know this will be right on the money for him.

"Oh ok. Well let me go so I can get on back. I hate that Atlanta traffic and I have to go downtown to reach the bus station."

I took the items and grabbed my phone and car keys before I made my way outside.

"Be careful Mommy," Justice yelled from across the street. She was sitting with her group of friends so I knew she wasn't trying to ride with me. I would just make sure that we spent some time together tomorrow since we hadn't in a few days. I owed her that.

Normally the trip from where we lived took me about an hour to get to Atlanta but since it was nearing rush hour I prepared myself to have some moments of immobility. Turning my radio on, it automatically connected to the car's Bluetooth. I hit the icon for Pandora and backed out. Justice must have been listening to music on my account because the song that was playing wasn't something that I had heard before. The beat was nice and the moment I looked up and saw her and her little crew standing on Cadence's porch dancing, I knew my assumptions were right.

Laughing, I threw my hand up and drove off. I listened to a few more of the songs on her playlist just to see what was being embedded into that spirit of hers. With the way this world was set up these days, music was a big influence on the youth and I didn't want my daughter exposed to certain things. I may not have been in church like a lot of people but no matter what had happened in my past I never stopped believing in God. I wasn't religious but I did trust Him. I can't lie and say that what happened with Corey and Kay wasn't the reason that I stopped going to church but it was. After that I had trouble trusting people who were supposed to lead me in the ways of The Lord so I felt better going on this journey by myself.

Mama told me that she understood how I felt but don't take forever to find another church home. She explained that a person being homeless didn't necessarily mean that they didn't have a place to rest their head but there was such thing as being spiritually homeless. I had begun to block everything out that had anything to do with church and its people immediately after I caught the two of them and it was draining now that I look back on it. As time went on and with prayer from my mama I got better. Her advice to me was to make sure that when I felt the tug to find a church home that I don't move on impulse, like I did when we started going to Greater Christian Tabernacle, but to move on purpose. Maybe if I had followed that logic years ago I could have avoided the hurt and pain. Or maybe that was all a part of God's plan. Who knows? He's just crafty like that I guess.

I skipped through the next few songs because they were just horrible until I found something that was more my speed. I was a 90's early 2000's R&B type of chick if I wasn't listening to gospel. Once I found something good and fell in line with the cars on the highway I was interrupted by my phone ringing. Looking down at the display I smiled hard seeing my favorite cousin's name and number.

"Heyyyyyy boo!" I squealed excitedly.

"Heyyyyyy Tink," Samson replied with just as much excitement. He was so extra but I loved that man.

"What's going on? I haven't heard from you in a while."

"I know boo. I been busy lately but I decided that I needed to come home for a visit. It's been too long."

Just hearing that he was coming home for a while got me even more excited. The last time I saw him was a week after I lost the baby and put Corey out. Samson came and wrecked shop. If the situation hadn't been so serious at the time it would have been hilarious but at that time I found nothing funny. All I did was egg him on when he ran down on Corey in the Walmart parking lot. See, Samson was a little flamboyant somebody and made no apologies for it. The way he fought was like he had been thugging in these streets all of his life and Corey was no match for him. But as soon as he heard those police sirens all of that thug flew right on out the window. This fool started flailing around on the ground like he wasn't the one that had just beat the breaks off of a 275-pound man. The whole scene was comical and by the end neither of them went to jail. Corey didn't bother pressing charges and the officers were too weak from laughing to take Samson seriously.

"When are you coming? God knows that I can't wait to see you."

"I know right? I'll be there in two weeks so take off 'cause we got lots of catching up to do," he said smacking his lips.

"When I go back to work next Wednesday I'll check to see how much time I have saved up."

"As much as you work you could probably take a whole year off."

"I don't work that much," I tried to defend myself.

"Girl bye! You think Auntie don't be giving me the tea. I know how much you work and the reason why but we'll get into that when I get there. How is my little baby?"

Sometimes I hated that my family knew me so well.

"She's doing good. Still making straight A's and even looking forward to doing the dual enrollment next school term."

"That's my girl. Well look I'll call you when I head out if not before. I gotta make sure I get pampered right and get some new outfits before I come into town slaying. You know y'all Georgia peaches don't know how to dress. I'm gonna show y'all how we get down in Chicago!"

I wanted to tell him to stop the madness because he knew good and well no one in Chicago dressed the way he did. They wouldn't be caught dead in any of his wardrobe. Samson dressed like he was blind but swore he stayed killing it. I couldn't wait to see what he popped up in and hear Uncle Cliff go in on him. I was going to make sure I borrowed one of his Depends 'cause I was sure to mess up my clothes peeing on myself from laughing.

"I'm sure you will have all eyes on you," I giggled.

"This would be true. I love you Tink," he said before we said out goodbyes and hung up.

I hadn't realized that I was almost to my destination. Between the music and my phone conversation I had made it in no time. After about another ten minutes I was pulling up in front of the Greyhound station. I got out and locked my doors before I remembered that I had no clue about who I was getting besides his name being Kiondre. Never once did I think to get a physical description so I called Ms. Myrtle.

"To God be the glory. This is the day that the Lord has made let us rejoice and be glad in it. Oh God! I feel your spirit Father. Yessuh!" Ms. Myrtle answered the phone in her usual manner. For as long as I had known her that had been her greeting.

She swore she was one of those real deep saints but would cuss you out in a heartbeat if you got wrong. That little old lady was a trip and her and my mama had been friends since she moved into the neighborhood a few years back. If I thought Mama and Uncle Cliff were bad at bickering, he and Ms. Myrtle were worse. I slick thought they had a thing for each other the way they carried on.

"Hey Ms. Myrtle it's Tayler. I'm here at the bus station but I don't know what your grandson looks like."

"Oh hey darling. Thank you again for going to pick him up."

"It's no problem. You know I don't mind."

"It's been a while since I saw my baby. He's about six one or six two and dark skin. I'm not sure if he has facial hair or not but look for someone that has a long scar on the left side of his face. It may not be real noticeable until you get up close cause I used to put money on his books so that he could get that good coco butter for it. I told him to use it twice a day and rub it into a circular motion. Coco butter works real good for stuff like that," she explained.

I was not trying to get a whole lesson on the benefits of coco butter and her instructions on how to use it so I tuned her out as I looked around the inside of the station. On my way in I didn't see anyone that even looked close to what she was describing so I moved deeper into the middle of the room. There were so many people inside that it was hard to focus. Mothers trying to calm down hungry and tired babies. People that looked like they were only there to get out of the outside elements and get some type of rest. My heart immediately went out to them because I knew that in a blink of an eye that could easily be me in their situation. I thanked God daily for things like that and for the ones that were still going through.

Moving through the sea of people I looked up just in time to see a man walk out of the men's room with his head down. He fit the description and height of what Ms. Myrtle told me so I walked a little closer. I didn't want to alarm him so I tried to see the left side of his face before I made myself known. I paid attention to the outfit that he was wearing and immediately I knew where he was coming from. The khaki pants, white tee, and white shoes let me know that he was fresh out the joint. This was the grandson that we heard so much about but I never knew his name until today or the reason he was locked up. It didn't matter because it wasn't my business and who was I to judge?

"I think I see him Ms. Myrtle, hold on," I told her before tapping him on his shoulder.

Turning around I made eye contact with one of the finest men I had ever set my eyes on. When he had come out of the bathroom I couldn't see his face too good because his head was down but looking at him in that moment, I knew God had sculpted this fine specimen with his bare hands. His arms were decorated with a few tattoos and I could tell that under his clothes was the body of a Greek god. My eyes traveled down his body and back again before I noticed the scar on his face. It had been years since a man had gotten my attention like this to where I was stuck on stupid.

"Can I help you?" he asked at the same time I heard Ms. Myrtle asking if I had found him.

Finally finding my voice I cleared my throat, yet I still struggled to get the words out.

"Umm, y-yes," I fumbled, "I'm Tay and your grandmother sent me to come and pick you up. She said that you had missed your bus."

Kiondre stared at me with an expression that I couldn't quite read and I was starting to get nervous.

"She's on the phone if you want to talk to her," I told him as I extended my hand out to him.

Looking down he reached for it and I could have sworn that I was about to pass out from the electricity that shot through my body when his hand touched mine. I did my best to hold in the shudder that my body was about to release but it didn't work. So, I had to play it off like I was cold and wrapped my arms around my body to make it look like I was warming myself up. The small smirk that flashed across his face didn't go unnoticed but he immediately caught himself and turned his attention to the conversation.

"Nannie?" he asked unsure. She must have confirmed that was her and I could see the rigidness begin to leave his body and relax.

"Nannie I told you that I could just catch the next one. You didn't have to send someone to come and get me. Yes ma'am. Alright, I'll see you in a little bit. I love you too Nannie and thank you," he ended the call and handed my phone back.

"You ready?" I asked him.

"I guess so," he chuckled lightly.

Why did it all of a sudden feel like every pair of eyes were on the two of us as we made our way to the exit?

"Oh here you go," I got his attention once we were inside of my car. I reached into the back seat and grabbed his food along with the drink. I'm glad that it was in the thermal bag because it should still be warm enough for him even after the drive.

"What's this?" he asked taking the stuff from my hand before closing his door and buckling his seat belt.

"When Ms. Myrtle called we were eating dinner so my mama packed you something. She figured that you might be hungry and needed something to sit on your stomach."

I sat looking out of my side view mirror waiting on the traffic to clear so that I could pull out and head back to the interstate. Out of the corner of my eye I could see a wide grin spread across his face and my heart fluttered. What in the world was going on with me? Maybe I needed a Snickers because I wasn't myself when I was hungry. I couldn't wait to get back to my mama's house so that I could eat and be back to my regular *I-don't-need-nor-want-a-man* self.

"Man this food is so on point," he spoke with his mouth full of chicken and greens. He was wasting no time with that yard bird because before I could get on I-75 good he was done.

"I'm sure it *was*. You should be sleep in the next fifteen minutes or so," I chuckled as I noticed him slide his seat back some to accommodate his tall frame.

"My bad. You don't mind if I move the seat do you?" he asked.

Fine and had manners. That chicken grease had left a nice little sheen on his full lips but not to the point where it looked like his lip gloss was poppin'. It was just enough to get my breath caught up again. I needed to get myself together.

I looked back at the road in order to concentrate because if I wasn't careful and wrecked while I lusted after this man I didn't know, I already knew that I was gonna be busting hell wide open.

Lord forgive me.

"I don't mind at all. I know you've been cooped up for long enough," I said and immediately wanted to take it back. The look on my face must have told him how embarrassed I was and he laughed.

"Don't trip. I know you didn't mean anything by it. Yes, I have been cooped up long enough, fifteen years to be exact, but I'm just thankful to be going home," he told me while he went back to adjusting his position and laying his head back.

"Well I know Ms. Myrtle is glad to have you back. Will you be staying there with her?" I asked even though I saw his eyelids beginning to droop.

"Only until I'm able to hopefully find a job and bring enough money in to move on my own. I know she won't mind me being there with her but it's time that I get my own."

Nodding my head, I turned the radio down some in order not to disturb him. As soon as he finished his last sentence he was out like a light. Every so often I would glance over at him and wonder what he had gone in for. He looked nice but looks were definitely deceiving. For him to say that he had been locked up for fifteen years that meant he had to be a teen when he went in because he looked to be around my age. I couldn't imagine being taken from my home and placed with a bunch of other people I didn't know. Some who were there for heinous crimes at that. Whatever it was hopefully he had been rehabilitated and didn't do anything to be sent back. So many times people, especially young black men, would get out of jail and go right back. They had become so institutionalized that jail was their comfort zone. They were welcomed right back considering how much money is made from people being incarcerated. Something had to change with this crooked system we had in place but until then I just prayed that Kiondre would be one of the few that had the motivation to stay on the right path.

Concentrating on the drive and stuck in my thoughts, I bobbed my head to the song that was playing low in the background as I drove. I didn't know how I was going to help him but I knew that something on the inside was telling me that I needed to.

Kiondre

I hadn't even realized that I had fallen asleep until I felt Tayler shake my arm. I jumped up so fast thinking that I was still on the inside and had allowed myself to fall too far into a deep sleep. When you weren't alert to your surroundings anyone could and would run up on you. They fed off of a person's vulnerability so I made it my business to never get caught off guard like that the whole fifteen years I was locked down. That's why I couldn't understand how I slept so hard. I know my body was thankful for it no matter what though.

"I'm sorry. I didn't mean to scare you. I just wanted to let you know we were here," Tayler said causing me to look into her beautiful face.

It was weird. The feelings that I was experiencing about a woman that I had just met. One would think that after fifteen years of being around nothing but men day in and day out that it was normal for a man to be attracted to the first woman that he saw once he was released. That may have been true for someone that had a normal life but my mother and the demons that she had bestowed upon me made sure that my life was anything but normal.

"Nah, you good. Just gotta get used to things again you know?" I asked her as I looked around at our surroundings.

The neighborhood was one that I wasn't familiar with being that my Nannie had moved years after I got locked up. I was kind of glad for that because I really wasn't up to running into anyone from my past although I knew that it was bound to happen sooner or later. Macon wasn't small but it wasn't big either. One good thing about it though, I knew that I had changed and grown over the years so the old Kiondre that they knew was no longer. I just wanted to live as normal as possible but something was telling me that was going to be easier said than done.

"Oh look at my baby!" I heard before I turned and looked in the direction of the voice. A smile as wide as the Nile spread across my face at the sight of my grandmother. I didn't know what she was doing to look the way she did but the woman before me hadn't aged since the last time I saw her. Looking at her no one would think that she had such a hard life and was almost in her seventies. Her long silver hair was cut into beautiful layers that stopped just past her shoulders, her copper colored skin was blemish and wrinkle free, and her hefty body fit well into the flowery dress that she wore.

"Hey Nannie," I greeted her once I got out of the car. Grabbing her around her waist I lifted her into the air as she gleefully laughed. Just the sound of her laughs made my eyes water and I couldn't help but to release the tears that formed.

I had never been the one to show my emotions or wear them on my sleeves but in that moment, I couldn't help it. I cried like a baby as I put her down but didn't remove myself from her embrace. The longer she held on to me the more I released everything that I was feeling.

"That's alright baby. Let it all out. It's all over now and God has given you another chance. Don't let your past keep you in bondage so that you can't move on to the future that is in store for you. You are not who you used to be or who they tried to make you out to be. Kiondre you are a child of the King and don't you ever forget that baby. You hear me?" my grandmother spoke into my ear as she cried with me. Words wouldn't form because of the lump that was in my throat so all I did was nod my head in response.

I knew that what she was telling me would be easier said than done but I was determined not to live in my yesterday but to strive towards my tomorrow. I felt that God had delivered me from my situation, now I just needed Him to deliver me from myself. The last thing I wanted was for my thoughts to consume me and I become my own worst enemy.

"Um, I'll let you go ahead and get situated and settled in. Is there anything else that I can do for the two of you before I go?" Tayler asked.

"Oh baby no," Nannie started as she let me go and wiped her face, "You have done so much already."

I wiped my own eyes before turning around and seeing Tayler standing behind us with tears of her own threatening to fall.

"Yeah I appreciate you taking time out of your day to come pick me up. Here let me at least give you some gas money," I told her reaching into my pocket.

"Kiondre that isn't necessary. I didn't do it for anything in return. I'm just glad that I was off and was available to do it," she said stopping me from giving her the money.

"At least let him take you out," Nannie said causing the both of us to snap our heads in her direction and look at her awkwardly. I knew what she was doing and she wasn't wasting any time trying to play matchmaker. I had only known Tayler existed for about two and a half hours and here this old woman was probably walking us down the aisle in her head already.

"Nannie I'm sure Tayler is a busy woman. How you gonna put us on the spot like that?" I tried laughing it off.

"Ms. Myrtle you think you slick huh?" Tayler laughed as well. I was glad that she wasn't uncomfortable or thrown off by what Nannie had said and her reaction eased the tension that I was starting to feel.

"What I do?" Nannie inquired innocently.

"If either of you need anything don't hesitate to call me. You can get my cell from Ms. Myrtle."

"Thanks again Tayler," I said to her.

"Call me Tay," she smiled before turning to get back into her car and pulling out of the yard. I didn't realize I was still watching her as she drove a few houses down and parked in the yard until Nannie spoke.

"That's her mother's house. She comes over all the time so you will see her again."

"I sure hope so," I said more to myself than her.

***

It had been a little over a week since I had been released and everyday my feet hit the pavement trying to apply for every job that I could. I was doing my best not to get discouraged each time I heard that I didn't have enough experience or that they would keep my application on file in case something opened up. I would have felt better if they would just be honest and tell me they wouldn't hire me because of my record because I knew that was the real reason. So many times a few of the guys on lockdown told me to not put that information on my applications but I just couldn't lie. It was bound to come out later so why not just be up front. I would rather get the job on the right terms instead of lying my way in. No matter how bad I needed and wanted a job I wasn't going to be deceitful in order to get it.

Standing at the bus stop I looked at the schedule and saw that I had another hour before the next bus came. My stomach reminded me that I had yet to feed it since the hearty breakfast that Nannie had made that morning. It was going on three in the afternoon and I was starving. I didn't see anywhere that I could get a quick bite from nearby so I pulled out the cell phone that Nannie insist I purchase. Times had changed so much and it took me almost two days to get the hang of how to use the touch screen. It was a trip that my grandma had to teach me everything I knew when it should have been the other way around.

Tapping the icon for the web I pulled up Google to try and search for some place close to eat when my phone flashed with a picture of Nannie.

"Hey beautiful," I greeted.

"Hey baby how did everything go?" she asked me with a voice full of anticipation. I hated to tell her that once again a day was coming to an end and I was still unemployed but I knew that she would only encourage me to continue.

"Same as the other days Nannie."

"Well that's alright baby. God will open the right door for you soon enough. Delayed does not meant denied. Oh to God be the glory!" she shouted and I smiled.

"Where are you now?" she continued.

"At the bus stop. I have like another hour before the next bus comes so I was going to try and find something to eat. I'm starving."

"Wait a minute," she told me before I heard what sounded like someone knocking on her door.

After a few moments she came back to the phone.

"Ki?"

"I'm still here Nannie."

"Tayler is on the way to get you. Where are you?" she asked.

Just the mention of Tayler had my stomach in knots and my forehead breaking out in a light sweat. I hadn't seen her since the day she dropped me off but Nannie explained that she worked a lot down at the hospital. I had even had the pleasure of meeting her mother and uncle who was a straight character.

"She doesn't have to do that Nannie. I'm good."

"Nonsense. Now tell me where you are."

Looking around I gave her the street name that I was on. Come to find out that she was just about to head in that direction to pick her daughter up from school and told me she would be there in about ten minutes. Hanging up the phone I stood and made sure that the black slacks were free of any lint or wrinkles and that my shirt and tie were on point. I had no idea why I was so pressed about how I looked. Maybe it was because of how I was dressed when we first met in the bus station. It wasn't much and far from being designer labels on my back but to me I looked pretty presentable. If my opinion of myself wasn't enough then all of the women that I had come into contact with since being home should have been. Sadly, their attempts of catching my eye didn't pay off for any of them. Sure, they were attractive, I just didn't have it in me to focus on them.

Beep. Beep.

Either Tayler drove like a bat out of hell or I was so into my thoughts that time slipped away from me. No matter how hard I tried not to smile I couldn't help it. Just the sight of her brought me so much happiness and I didn't understand it. I shouldn't be feeling like this. My mother made sure to direct me down the avenue that she said she knew I was already headed in. One where women didn't travel.

Shaking those thoughts away I got in the car and put my seat belt on before she pulled off.

"I appreciate you coming to get me. Again."

"You're welcome. I just got off and happened to stop by to see if Nannie needed anything before I came to get Justice."

"Justice?"

"My daughter," she told me as her face lit up. I could tell that her daughter was her world just by the look on her face. It made me think about my own child.

"Here." Just like before Tayler had brought me something to eat just when I needed it.

I thanked her before reaching into the Zaxby's bag and pulling the food out. Opening my Zax sauce, I starting dipping the hot fries in it and sending it straight to my mouth. I didn't care how hot the food was at the moment I just needed it in my stomach.

"Man it's been forever since I had some Zaxby's."

"I love that place," was all she said before she pulled into the line that was formed in front of what I assumed was her daughter's school.

By the time we made it to the front I was done eating and drinking the last of my coke. I watched as hundreds of kids made their way to a car, bus, or just standing around laughing with their friends. The joy they had displayed on their faces was something that I couldn't relate to. Even when I was in school before I went to jail there was no joy. All of the things that I should have experienced as a child was stripped from me from the age of four and I never got it back. The constant bullying I received from my peers because of how I looked and added to the abuse that I endured from my mother took all of that away from me.

"That must be your daughter?" I asked noticing the young lady that was heading in our direction with a friend in tow. She was Tayler's twin so they had to be related.

"We look that much alike huh?" she laughed.

"Twins."

I reached for the door to get out and get in the back seat but was stopped by the younger version of Tayler.

"You don't have to move. We can get in the back," Justice giggled along with her friend.

"Hey Mommy."

"Hey TeeTee."

The girls got in and greeted Tayler before turning their attention back to me.

"Are you Ms. Myrtle's grandson?" Justice asked.

"That would be me. It's nice to meet you," I let her know before giving her a warm smile.

"You too. This is my best friend Cadence." Justice introduced her friend.

"Hi," Cadence waved and smiled.

"Hi darling," I greeted before turning around.

"Ma you brought me something to eat?" Justice asked.

"That was Kiondre's food greedy girl."

"Why I gotta be all that?"

"Cause you have been greedy since birth," Cadence joked.

"Shut up!"

"Lord these two here," Taylor said shaking her head and laughing.

I sat quietly and observed the three of them and how they responded to one another as we rode. The bond that they shared was nothing like I had ever seen but it was enjoyable. Once we were back in the neighborhood Tayler stopped to drop off her daughter's friend before stopping at Nannie's house.

"I'll see you later sis."

"Ok," Justice replied.

"Bye Tee Tee."

"See you in a little bit boo," Tayler told her.

"Nice meeting you Mr. Kiondre," she said getting out.

"You too sweetheart."

There was something familiar about the young girl but I couldn't put my finger on it. She didn't look like anyone that I knew right off hand but it was something. Maybe she was related to someone I grew up with back in the day. Who knew? It wasn't important and I wasn't going to pry.

We watched her as she walked up on the porch and was greeted by a man that looked to be around my age. He had a scowl on his face that didn't sit well with me. It was a scowl that I had seen on too many occasions by my mother. She didn't seem to be affected by his presence but it still bothered me. I said a quick prayer in my head for her safety although I didn't know why but I knew that she needed it. Maybe I was overreacting and maybe I wasn't.

"Ugh. I'll be glad when Sheba wakes up and leaves his behind," Tayler spoke with so much attitude.

Sheba? Why did that name sound so familiar to me?

"We just gotta keep praying for them Mama. God will work it out for them," Justice encouraged as we pulled off.

"Let me know if you need anything. I'm off this weekend so I'll be free," Tay told me just before I got out.

I didn't know if she was just being nice or if she was actually giving me a hint that she would be available but I decided to try anyway.

"You want to go get a drink or something this weekend? I mean it's the least I can do since you looked out for me more than once."

Time stood still as I waited for her to respond. Why was I nervous?

"She'll be ready tomorrow at eight, right Mama?" Justice stepped in and answered for her.

"Ye-yeah. Tomorrow is cool," she stammered causing me to smile. She was nervous too and that somehow made me feel a little better.

"Cool. I'll see you then." I hurriedly spoke before getting out of the car and making my way inside. I looked back once to wave before she finally pulled off causing me to laugh at the expression that was plastered over Justice's face. If I didn't know any better I would think she was in cahoots with Nannie on trying to set me and her mother up. Shaking my head I made my way inside to prepare myself mentally for tomorrow.

Tayler

It was going on seven thirty and I was still sitting on my bed in my old terrycloth bathrobe that had seen better days. I don't know why I was so nervous but ever since Kiondre had asked me out I was trying to find reasons to back out. Not that he wasn't attractive or it was hard being around him but because it was too easy to be around him. It had only been a few weeks but the times we were together it was like we had known each other all of our lives. I was falling and I knew that wasn't good. Especially since I had sworn off dating from the time I signed my divorce papers. I just didn't want to deal with another heartbreak and if I didn't date then it couldn't get that far. But then Kiondre entered my life and changed the game on me.

"I'll get it!" I heard Justice yell after the doorbell rang. I wasn't expecting anyone and people knew not to just pop up at my house without calling. I would literally sit in the living room with my front door open and watch people ring my bell while looking in their face if they did not get an invite. So whoever it was should have been lucky that I was a ball of nerves and Justice was home.

"Juss who is it?" I screamed from my closet. I had to pick Kiondre up since he wasn't familiar with the area we were going to so I knew that it wasn't him. Besides I never told him where I lived.

"Ma!" Justice yelled a few seconds later. I knew my child so I could tell by the tone of her voice with just that one word, whoever was at the door was about to piss me off.

Heading down the stairs with a scowl on my face I couldn't help but to deepen it the moment I saw my ex-husband standing on the other side of the door.

"This how you gonna treat your Daddy?" Corey asked Justice like he was really offended.

"Did my daddy care how he treated his daughter and his wife?" she clapped back at him.

I understood she was still upset with Corey but as bad as I hated to admit it he was still an adult and her father. There was one thing that I didn't play around with and that was my child disrespecting an adult. She had every right to be mad but I wouldn't let her talk out the side of her neck with him but before I could chastise her he opened his mouth causing me to almost let her go in on him.

"This how you raising my daughter? I knew I should have filed for full custody. Who was I kidding to think that someone of your caliber could raise a child right," he had the nerve to scoff.

"Justice go to your room," I said and she already knew what time it was. With one last roll of her eyes she turned and motioned for Cadence to follow her up the stairs.

I took the time it would take her to make it to her room to calm myself down before I spoke. It didn't work though because as soon as I heard her door slam I went off.

"You bastard! You have some nerve trying to come over here and speaking on anything I do here especially raising the daughter that you walked out on!" I was livid and if I didn't calm down and fast, I was about to give him one good old fashioned cursing out.

"I have the right to speak on what I see Tayler. Her nasty attitude is one that is reflective of the whore who pushed her out. You must have forgotten how we met," he said as a smug grin made its way across his face.

"Oh I definitely remember how we met and if I had known that this would have been the hell I had to pay for that night then trust me, I would have run in the opposite direction. Being fourteen and young and dumb I thought I knew what I was doing but I was so wrong. So if that was a dig to try and embarrass me about the woman that I once was then you wasted your time. My past doesn't define my now or my future. You are the one that wants to act like your past is squeaky clean. Yes I did things at a young age like drugs, was shaking my butt in a club I had no business being in, and sleeping with a man that was older than me. Even had our daughter before I had been able to experience my sixteenth birthday. I hate to break it to you though I'm no longer bothered by any of that. See unlike you, I accept the person that I used to be because it helped me to be the woman that I am today. But you on the other hand are still in denial. God was the one who made it possible for you to shake that habit because not everyone makes it out. Just because you got a fancy law degree doesn't mean that you didn't suck on that glass d-," I paused before I came undone completely. From the look on Corey's face I didn't need to continue. He already knew where I was heading.

"Do me a favor," I continued. "Don't come around here anymore. You made your choice when you cheated on me and caused us to lose our baby. You embarrassed our family and broke the vows that you made to God so the least you could do is be there for your daughter but you can't even do that. Go back to your flavor of the week and leave us alone Corey."

Slamming the door in his face without giving him the chance to respond, I stood there for a few minutes to get myself together. It was crazy how before I found out that Corey was cheating on me he was the man of my dreams. But once his secrets were out in the open I couldn't stand the sight of him. His attitude had gotten so nasty and everything that my mama saw in him from the beginning had begun to surface. Agnes knew she had a powerful gift of discernment and I wished I had listened to her.

My mood had changed just that fast and I didn't even feel like going out anymore. I had Corey to thank for that. I knew Kiondre would probably be disappointed but hopefully he would get over it. Just as I was walking away from the door I saw Justice and Cadence coming back downstairs before the doorbell rang again. Now see since Corey was trying my patience he was about to catch these hands.

"If you don't get the hell away from my house!" I yelled snatching the door open as I fumed.

"Dang Tink its like that?" my cousin Samson sashayed his way into the house.

"Cousin!" Justice yelled once she saw him and ran up to him.

"Ohhhh look at you Baby Tink looking all cute and whetnot!" he said to her as he stuck his tongue out and did some dance where he looked like a chicken that was getting its neck rung. That boy knew he had no rhythm but swore he could dance. And lets not even get on how he dressed.

Samson put me in the mind of that Instagram comedian that I followed. His real name was Kway but he portrayed this character named TiTi. From the facial expressions that Samson made to the makeup and crazy hair that he wore you would think they were twins. I watched him doing his best to twerk alongside Justice and Cadence and couldn't help but to laugh. His outfit of choice was the most hilarious thing I have ever witnessed.

He was wearing a pair of bright neon tights on his rail thin legs making them look like glow sticks, an *ugly* flowered shirt with ruffles around the neck and sleeves, and some of those plastic flip flops with the bow on the top that I was positive came from a beauty supply store. I didn't know if he was allergic to or scared of lotion but the way his ankle all the way down to his toes was covered in a thick coating of ash, clearly he didn't believe in it. But that had nothing on what rested on his head.

This *whole fool* had the audacity to have what looked like he had cut up three different lace fronts and pieced them together like a puzzle that didn't fit. Cause baby they were definitely forced. The left side of his head looked like a newborn panda had decided to hibernate while the back was a part of a braided wig that swooped around to the right side. Oh God, that right side! I couldn't tell if my cousin had glued on 13 pieces of a 27 piece or if it was previously a wig. The lace was showing because he hadn't trimmed it down like it needed and the light color clashed with his dark skin. It was just a mess but I loved my cousin something serious.

"So it's just forget me huh?" I asked closing the door and moving towards them.

"It shole is cause of that little funky attitude you had when I opened the door. That is no way to address a queen," he flipped his head dramatically and walked off to the couch.

"You know I would never intentionally have an attitude with you boo. I thought you were Corey." I explained.

Why did I mention that man's name?

"Corey who? I know good and well you don't mean that punk that you used to be married to with the one little ear," he stated with a hard roll of the eyes.

"You wrong for that Samson," I fell out laughing because it was true. Corey was real sensitive about that short ear and would always try to grow his hair long enough to make it unnoticeable. He was a handsome man so it didn't bother me when we had met. Samson got on to him every time he saw Corey and didn't care how he felt about it.

"You know its true. Ear so little he can't even wear ear buds 'cause it will fall out with his ugly self. I bet when his mammy used to tell him 'If you can huh, you can hear' he got a whipping for not responding. Behind really couldn't hear. So what he want?" Samson was too much.

I was laughing so hard with the girls that it took me a good five minutes to gather myself before I could answer him.

"I don't know what he wanted because we didn't get that far. He came out his mouth slick and I went off on him."

"He better be glad I was stuck in traffic or he would have caught this hot two piece I still got for him."

"You did enough damage last time cuz."

"Well he better come correct or stay away if he can't get himself together and act like he got some sense. Anyway, what y'all doing tonight?"

"Mommy has a date," Justice's big mouth blurted out.

"Not anymore. I'ma bout to call and cancel. After dealing with your father I don't even want to be bothered."

"I know you lying! No ma'am you will not let that dwarf ear, I-can't-hear-you-talk-into-my-good-ear low life cause you to continue to put your dating life on hold. Baby we about to get you right tonight," Samson spoke as he sat on the couch like he was twerking on the couch. Just stiff as a board.

"What you mean get me right?" I wanted to know. My eyebrow was arched so high it was about to hit the ceiling fan. I knew he wasn't talking about dressing me. If that was the case I might as well stay home because I would not be going anywhere in one of his creations.

"I'm about to go find you a bomb outfit, get that hair right, and beat that face hunty yezzz!" he squealed excitedly.

"No!" Justice, Cadence, and I all yelled out simultaneously.

"Why? I know y'all see how I'm dressed. I stay killing the game," Samson got up and pranced around the living room. If he popped his hip too much he was gonna break it.

"Yeah we see you and you definitely killed an animal and put it on your head," Cadence mumbled low enough just for me and Juss to hear her. It took everything in my power not to laugh but Justice took the cake.

"Hello PETA? Yes we need you to come and get our cousin because he killed a baby panda and used it's fur to make him a quick weave," my child said with a straight face as she held her phone up to her ear.

"Ahhhhh!" I screamed as I fell completely on the floor. Justice was most definitely my child with that sense of humor. The look on Samson's face was priceless as he glared at the three of us laughing with tears falling from our eyes.

"Whatever. I know what I'm doing so come on," he instructed walking towards the stairs. God knows I needed the strength to get up and follow because I was so weak and out of breath.

"Oh unt uh Ma come on. We gotta make sure he doesn't throw anything together and have you looking crazy."

Agreeing with her I got up and followed behind. I guess I was going on this date after all. I just prayed that it was worth it.

Kiondre

"Andrews you got a visitor."

I rolled over on my back and just stared at the guard behind the cell bars. It was my twenty first birthday and I hadn't had a visitor since the judge had given me my sentence. My grandma tried visiting but I had asked her to stop coming because it hurt more to see her with tears in her eyes all because of a decision that was kind of made for me. Something inside of me told me that I shouldn't go down to the visiting room but against my better judgement I slowly got up and moved towards him.

After he secured my wrists in the cuffs, I moved out of the tiny space and walked alongside him until we got to the first security door. With each step I took it felt like the walls were closing in around me and I couldn't understand why. That was until I walked into the large room and my eyes landed on the last person that I wanted to see. The anger that I felt rising up in me was one that I was very familiar with and had taken me a long time to suppress. But looking into a pair of eyes that were just like mine brought those familiar feelings back.

"The enemy looks for a reaction. If you don't give him one he can't use it against you. He won't leave you alone completely and will try another avenue to get what he is looking for. You are stronger than you were when you came in here. Walk in that and show him who's really in control," I heard the guard speak from beside me and the torment inside of me begin to subside. It wasn't many guards in there that actually treated the inmates like they were still humans instead of animals but there was a few. I had

been fortunate enough to have encountered the ones that saw past my crime.

Nodding my head I walked over to the table that was assigned for this visit and sat down, never letting my eyes break contact with the person who was before me.

"You look good son. How are you?" my mother asked as her eyes roamed from the top of my head to my chest and back up since the rest of my body was hidden behind the table.

I hated when she did that because there was always something behind her eyes that made me uncomfortable. She would always look at me like that right before she allowed her demons to torture me.

"Why are you here?" I wanted to know as I ignored her question.

"It's your twenty first birthday baby. You know what that means right?"

Looking at her I could feel my forehead beginning to dip in the middle and my nose begin to flare.

"Calm down Kiondre. She can't hurt you here." I did my best to give myself a silent pep talk so that I wouldn't go off on her.

"What does it mean?" I asked.

"Did you forget?"

I had no idea what she was talking about and I was tired of playing this question and answer game with her. She needed to spit out the reason she was here so that I could go back and sleep my day away. Right before I told her just that the revelation hit me.

"You're coming home KiKi!" she said excitedly like that was a good thing causing me to frown.

"Don't call me that," I mumbled. I hated when she called me that and she knew it.

"That's your name," she replied with her loving tone slowly slipping away. The nasty attitude that she tried to hide was beginning to surface quicker than she wanted it to. I could tell by the way her face tried to soften. "I'm sorry. Happy Birthday son and I can't wait for you to come home with me,"

"Why?"

"What do you mean why? I miss my child and you shouldn't be here in the first place."

"You don't miss me you just miss what I could do for you!" I yelled even though I didn't mean to.

"Boy who are you raising your voice at? I'm your mother and you will respect me as such," she spoke through gritted teeth causing me to laugh but there was no humor in it.

"Respect? Respect? You don't even know what that word is. When did you ever respect me? Huh?"

"You are the child and I am the parent so I don't have to respect you but you will respect me. Do you understand me? I raised you," she ranted.

"You raised me to be gay! You raised me to sleep with the men of your church for money and you want me to respect you? How in the hell do you expect me to respect a woman who should have protected her child from people like that? Mama you sold my body when I was five years old to Deacon Johnson. Do you have

any idea what it feels like to experience pain like that? No child should go through that!" I felt my pressure rising, the tears falling, and the stares from everyone in the room but I didn't care. This was the first time that I had ever told her how I felt and I didn't care how she took it.

"You little bastard! I was all you had when your no-good daddy decided that he didn't want to be a father. Because of you he left me since I wouldn't get an abortion like he said. That meant I had to figure out how to take care of you on my own. I was tired of selling my body to feed your little ass so it was time for you to take care of me."

"Take care of you? I was a child! How do you expect me to take care of you when that's your job? Maybe if you had kept your legs closed we both would have been better off!" I yelled at her.

Whap!

I didn't even flinch when she slapped me across my face because that pain was nothing compared to the internal pain I dealt with on the daily.

"Get her out of here!" Officer Harvey yelled to one of his co-workers as he grabbed me and ushered me out of the room. Just like when I entered the room my eyes never left her as we were carried in opposite directions. It was in that moment that I knew God Himself would have to get down off of His throne to tell me to forgive her. Even then He would have to do some heavy convincing. If the next time I saw her was on Judgement Day it would be too soon and even then I would rather burst hell wide open if that meant spending an eternity never seeing her again. Then again her soul was so rotten she would be burning too.

Once I got back to my cell I exploded.

"I hate her! Why me God? Huh? This isn't love! You let her snatch my soul from me. She didn't protect me and neither did you. What kind of God are you?" I screamed before beating my head on the cement wall repeatedly.

BOOM! BOOM! BOOM!

"Kiondre! Kiondre baby wake up!" I heard Nannie yelling.

Sitting up quickly I sucked in all of the air that I could because it felt like it was being depleted by the second.

"Calm down baby. Breath slow. I got you baby," she said as she pulled me close and held me tight as we cried together. "I don't care what the enemy tells you son you are not what your mother tried to make you out to be. You are a child of the Most High God and although the circumstances may not look like He loved you, trust me baby He does."

I heard everything she was saying to me but I couldn't agree with her at that moment. My heart and mind were in a battle with each other. Both telling me two different things and I didn't know which one was right. Maybe both, maybe neither. I just didn't know.

"Get your stuff ready for your shower so you can get dressed," Nannie said to me once I was able to calm myself down.

"For what? I just want to try and rest Nannie."

"Oh no sir. I know this is tough but I can't and I won't let you stay in here and let your thoughts get the best of you. You are going to be ready when Tayler gets here in a little bit and you will go out and have a good time. It's for you to start living and not just existing. The both of you."

I had totally forgotten about my date with Tayler and I really didn't want to be around her after being drug back into my past. Part of me wasn't feeling it but part of me still wanted to be in her presence. It was like when she was around I was at peace. Wiping my hand across my face to remove the moisture of my tears, I stood up and did as I was told. The whole time I showered and dressed I did something that I hadn't in a long time. I prayed. If I was going to get through this night I needed someone stronger than me to guide me. By the time I had finished putting my foot into my loafer and snapping on my watch I heard the doorbell ring.

"Here goes nothing," I told myself before leaving my bedroom and heading to the front of the house.

Tayler

I pulled up to Ms. Myrtle's house a little after eight and I was hoping that Kiondre still wanted to go out. Once I let Justice, Cadence, and Samson get me together my spirits had picked up tremendously. I was looking too good to stay in the house and someone was gonna see all of this beauty.

Getting out of the car I walked up to their porch and rung the bell then waited.

"Here I come!" I heard Ms. Myrtle yell from the other side before the locks clicked and we came face to face with one another.

"What's wrong?" I asked her as I looked down at my body.

"Girl where you been hiding all that at?" she laughed causing me to join in.

The red two-piece skirt and top set that I wore fit my body like a glove. My stomach wasn't flat but it wasn't huge either so I could get by with the look. The top exposed my shoulders and stopped just above my belly button. The hem of the skirt landed right below my knees showing off my pretty legs and the gold strappy heels that I wore set the outfit off perfectly. I had gold accessories on and decided to pull my hair up on top of my head instead of letting it be down. I wanted to possibly go dancing and I didn't want to be hot all night.

"Am I overdressed?" I asked realizing that we never discussed where we were going and what we should wear.

Suite Lounge in Atlanta was the spot I wanted to take him to. I took into consideration that he had missed so much and I didn't want to overwhelm him with too much too soon. Where we were going was a mixture of a laid-back atmosphere and a little turn up if you wanted. The bottom half people could sit and have a nice relaxing meal and drink with some dancing and live singing. Then if you wanted a little more the upstairs had bottles popping and wall to wall people. If Kiondre wanted to experience them both then we would.

Before she could answer me movement from behind her caused me to look in that direction with a smile creeping across my face. Lord this man was fine. My eyes traveled the length of his body starting at the way his red polo styled shirt rested against his big body. Next they landed on the nice khaki slacks he wore and then to the tan loafers with the gold buckle on the front. Once I was relieved that he wasn't under or overdressed my eyes made their way back to his face. Brother man had already gotten his hair cut and beard trimmed which I noticed earlier in the day but the way he was looking at me caused me to blush. He was definitely enjoying his view of me but there was something else in his eyes. I didn't know what it was but I knew that just like me, he was in need of a good time.

"Look at y'all matching and everything," Ms. Myrtle spoke up causing the both of us to laugh at the fact that we were both stuck on one another and forgot she was even in the room.

That was the first time that I realized that we were indeed matching. From the colors to the accessories we definitely looked like a couple.

"You look beautiful," Kiondre sad walking over to me and shocking me by taking my hand in his.

There goes that electricity again.

"You do too. Um, I mean you look handsome as well," I corrected myself. The smile that his lips made reached his eyes and I knew it was genuine.

Most of the times when men looked at me like that I could tell they only wanted one thing from me which I wasn't about to give to any of them. But the way Kiondre looked and made me feel let me know that whatever he was feeling was for real and I appreciated that for once.

"When I asked you out earlier I wasn't thinking about the fact that I didn't know of anywhere to take you," he admitted with a hint of embarrassment on his face.

"Don't worry I got us covered. If you don't mind a little ride before we get there I'm sure you'll enjoy it."

"I'm sure as long as he's with you he will enjoy it," Ms. Myrtle stepped in and answered for him.

"Go to bed Nannie," Kiondre laughed.

"Oh no I'm not. I'm gonna call Agnes and get to planning this here wedding. So gone on," she said as serious as a heart attack.

"What?" we both asked in unison.

Instead of responding to us Ms. Myrtle just pushed us out the front door before locking it behind us.

"Did that really just happen?" I chuckled.

"That old woman is a mess," he laughed. "Here let me help you."

Moving in front of me without letting my hand go Kiondre led me down the steps and to my car. I hit the locks and let him open my door for me before getting in and closing the door. I watched as he walked around the front of the car looking like a chocolate god.

"Jesus help me and these thoughts," I prayed out loud right before he opened the passenger side door and got it. He smelled so good that I wanted to just sniff his neck.

"So where we going?" he asked me taking me away from my thoughts.

"It's a nice spot called Suite Lounge. It's in Atlanta but it won't take us too long to get there unless you want to go somewhere close."

"Nah that's fine. The longer I get to spend with you the better."

I didn't know what to say in response to that but I was all smiles as I pulled out of the yard and made my way down the street. I blew my horn at my uncle sitting on the front porch with one of his friends and headed out of the neighborhood.

***

"How many?" the hostess asked at the front door of the lounge.

It was a nice little crowd for a Friday night. Not too many people like the few times when I had been in the past.

"Just two," Kiondre stepped up and told her before she picked up two menus and walked us further inside.

"Will this work for you?" she turned to us to get our approval of the booth she stopped us in front of.

"Yes thank you."

"I figured you would want to get a little cozy with bae," she whispered in my ear causing me to blush. I didn't know what to say to that so I just nodded and slipped into the seat. "Your server will be right over."

"This spot is nice. Nothing like I expected," Kiondre told me as he looked around.

"What did you expect?" I wanted to know.

Shrugging his shoulders he sat back before he spoke.

"I'on know. Considering that this is my first time ever in a club I guess I expected it to be like what I've seen on tv or heard from the other inmates. Wall-to-wall people everywhere, women scantily dressed with men trying to pull anything in a skirt and a few fights breaking out."

I hadn't even thought about this being his first time in a club. Since he had been in jail from the time he was a teen until recently, he had missed a lot of the things that by now I had gotten out of my system. It may have seemed small to someone else who had the joy of experiencing their freedom but to someone like him this was big. I could tell that by the look in his eyes that he was thinking just that.

"Well allow me to show you a good time tonight then. I don't really go out too much anymore but I don't think I forgot how to party," I laughed causing him to smile just as our server for the night came over.

"Good evening, my name is Walt and I'll be your server for the night. Can I start the two of you off with something to drink?"

"May I?" I asked Kiondre. I didn't want to offend him by just stepping in and ordering for him since that was something that my father used to always do for my mama. Since it was his first time drinking I didn't want him ordering something that would cause me to have to try and carry his big self to the car.

"Absolutely," he answered showing me that gorgeous smile of his while bobbing his head to the music.

"Can we get two of your Presidential 12's and two glasses of water please?"

"Sure thing. Do you need a few more minutes to look over the menu?"

"I know what I want but do you need some more time?" I looked to him and inquired.

"Nah I know what I want but you can go first beautiful."

Every time he called me that I could tell that he meant it giving me just a little more confidence. It had been so long that I just stopped caring about my appearance or how people looked at me because I focused on work and coming straight home. It wasn't like I never got complimented by men but I could look at them and tell they only wanted one thing. Kiondre was different.

"I'll get the salmon tacos and a jumbo lump crab cake please," I ordered.

"And let me get the chicken and waffles," Kiondre spoke before we handed our menus over and waited for the server to return with our drinks.

We made small talk and relaxed while listening to the smooth sounds of the '90's R&B that played through large building. The drinks that were brought to us had mellowed the two of us out and conversation flowed as if we had been friends forever. By the time our food was delivered we had both had two drinks a piece and felt like we were about to starve.

"Lord I been waiting all day to eat," I said as my food was placed in front of me.

"Nervous about tonight?" he asked me 'causing me to wonder how he knew the exact reason of me missing all of my meals. "I didn't eat because I was nervous too."

The two of us laughed at one another before saying grace and digging in to our plates.

"Mmph," Kiondre grunted.

"Good?" I asked taking another bite of my food.

"You have no idea."

It took us no time to finish before we were both good and full. The crowd was starting to pick up and the song selections were a little more current. The few drinks that I had indulged in had me feeling right so I threw my hands in the air as I bobbed my head to Kehlani's *Distraction.*

"Are you down to be a distraction baby?" I sang along causing Kiondre to laugh.

I knew I wasn't the best singer in the world but I thought I was on American Idol at the moment and no one could tell me any different.

"Let's dance," he suggested not waiting for me to agree before he grabbed my hand and gently pulled me behind him out of the booth. He pulled out enough to cover our meal as well as a tip. I kind of felt bad that he was spending money that he needed to save but he insisted on it so I let it go.

Maneuvering through the crown we made our way to the dance floor and tried our best to find a good spot to where we weren't bumping into anyone. Just as we were passing a group of men one of them grabbed my causing me to snatch away and give him a nasty look. It wasn't because he was unattractive but I hated when men felt that they had the right to just touch a woman whenever he wanted to especially when he didn't know her. What was wrong with just smiling and speaking then let her decide if she wants to entertain him?

"Gone then!" he yelled out over the music like that would move me and make me change my mind.

Turning around I followed behind Kiondre until he stopped and turned to pull me close and spun me around. My back was facing him as his arms slid around my waist. The scent of his cologne crept up my nose and I felt like I was being hypnotized. Rocking back and forth to the music it felt like we were the only two people in the building and I didn't want that feeling to end. Unfortunately, it did the moment I looked up.

I had been feeling like someone was watching me the whole time I danced and I did my best to discretely look around without Kiondre noticing. Looking to my left and then my right I didn't see anyone paying us any attention until I looked straight ahead. The dude from earlier was still standing in the same place holding up the wall with one of the nastiest looks I had ever seen on someone.

"You know him?" Kiondre asked catching me off guard and never once stopping the movement of his body behind mine.

"Not at all. I guess he still in his feelings from me not stopping when he tried to get my attention earlier."

Deciding to ignore him, I turned my attention back to my date for the night. The music switched up again and before I knew it we were both tired and ready to go. It wasn't even midnight and I was ready to go. I was so glad that he felt the same way since I was the one who had to drive back home. The liquor in my system had worn off but I still didn't like driving too late at night.

Just as we made our way out of the door and to the parking lot all hell broke loose.

"Aye!" we heard come from behind us to see the same guy from earlier and two of his friends coming towards us. "Don't I know you?"

At first I thought that he was taking to me but then I saw that his eyes were focused on Kiondre. Looking between the two men I silently prayed that nothing escalated but I don't think that prayer made it to the Kingdom.

"Nah," was all Kiondre said.

The way he stepped to the side in order to shield me with his body made me smile on the inside. If I wasn't already team Kiondre before I definitely was at that moment.

"You sure about that?" the man asked.

"He said no already," I spoke up agitated. No one had time to be playing games with him. Besides my bladder was letting me know I needed to find a bathroom and fast.

Looking over to me the man never let the menacing look leave his face.

"Aye man shut up," he said to me.

My neck snapped back so fast that it should have fallen off my shoulders. Before I could respond, because I was definitely going to respond, Kiondre spoke.

"Listen bruh, I don't know who you are but if you speak to my lady like that again it's gone be some problems."

"So nigga you done been in jail and now you think you got balls? Where were them balls when yo' mama had you out here suck-," he started but never got the chance to finish before Kiondre hit him with a right hook that made him stumble back and land on the ground.

Before homeboy could even gather himself Kiondre had pounced on him like a lion did a gazelle. Every time his punches would land he spoke like my mama would when she would give me whippings.

"If. I. Said. I. Didn't. Know. You. Then. I. Don't. Know. You."

The man's friends were either caught off guard like I was or they wanted no parts of what Kiondre was delivering because they just stood there until security began approaching. I shook my head as I watched them do their best to grab Kiondre but he was too strong.

"Kiondre! Stop!" I yelled and immediately he obliged. It was as if he had blacked out until he heard my voice. The look in his eyes let me know that that wasn't a side of him that he wanted me to see.

His chest heaved up and down as the security guards grabbed each of the men trying to find out what was going on until we saw the blue lights. My heart dropped to my stomach at the thought of Kiondre going back to jail and the way he was looking I knew he thought it was over for him too.

"What's going on here?" one of the officers asked. He looked like he woke up every morning just to lock people up for breathing wrong and it had me shook.

"I don't know how these three got in the club when they were banned from here. We were coming out to have them removed from the property when we saw the fight happening," the guard explained.

"Tayler?" I heard my name. Looking around I noticed the other officer immediately.

"Joseph. Oh thank God it's you," I said relieved.

Joseph had been a friend of Corey's for as long as I could remember. Considering the fact that my ex was a criminal lawyer he worked constantly with the police and he and Joseph had become good friends. He and his wife would come over sometime for dinner and vice versa. When they found out that Corey had cheated on me their relationship was somewhat a thing of the past. Karen, Joseph's wife, would reach out to me every now and then to check on Justice and me but that was as far as it went.

"What happened?" he asked me with genuine concern.

"We don't even know these men. One of them tried to grab my attention earlier and I wouldn't entertain him. So when it was time to leave he followed us out here. I thought that maybe he was coming out here because of me but then he started talking real reckless out of his mouth towards my date. Next thing I know they were fighting."

"Alright. You two hold tight," Joseph told us leaving to go to the other men who were still being restrained.

"Are you ok?" Kiondre asked me.

"I should be asking you that. Look at your hands."

He had beat that man so bad that his knuckles were swollen.

"I can't believe I'm about to go right back to jail,"

I knew that he was worried about returning to the place that he had just left but if I could do anything about it he wouldn't have to worry about that.

"It looks like the three of them are saying that you were the one to attack Mr. Long first. Is this true?" the other officer that was with Joseph asked. He already had his handcuffs out and ready to read Kiondre his rights.

"Yeah. I hit him first," Kiondre stated calmly.

"Turn around and place your hands behind your back."

"It wasn't his fault!" I yelled making Joseph turn around with a confused look on his face. "Joseph it isn't his fault. They followed behind us and provoked him."

"Stand down or you'll be going with him."

"It's not his fault," another security guard spoke up on behalf of Kiondre. "He was just enjoying his night with his lady. These three were trespassing anyway. Had they not been here this would have never happened."

"Uncuff him," Joseph ordered.

With a loud huff Officer Prick did as he was told before giving Kiondre a stern look and walking off.

"Don't worry about anything Tay. Y'all drive safe," Joseph told us before going back to his car that held two of the men before pulling off ahead of the other patrol car.

"Thank you God," I sighed before getting in my own car followed by Kiondre.

For the first thirty minutes neither of us said a word because we were both in our own thoughts. I wondered what the man was about to say before Kiondre hit him. It made me think that Kiondre in fact did know who he was and whatever he was about to say wasn't something that I was supposed to know.

"I'm sorry that you had to see me like that," Kiondre spoke just above a whisper. I could hear the embarrassment in his voice.

"It wasn't your fault. He started with you. Thank you for protecting me though before things got crazy."

"That's what a man is supposed to do right?" The smile that he wore was one of uncertainty.

I decided not to say anything else when he closed his eyes and leaned his head back on the head rest. He flexed his hands and I noticed his jaws tighten when he did. Don't ask me what made me reach over and grab his left hand to begin gently massaging it. The tension in his body began to ease although he flinched a couple of times. Kiondre was looking at me, I could feel it, but I kept my eyes on the road. The way my heart was pounding I knew that if I looked at him we would be on the side of '75 somewhere.

We finally pulled in to Ms. Myrtle's yard and I put the car in park. It was almost comical how the two of us were sitting like teens who were on their first date. We were so quiet you could hear a rat peeing on cotton.

"Make sure you let me know when you get home," he spoke up first breaking the silence.

"I will. Thank you for tonight."

"No, thank you. I know it may not have ended well but if you'd let me I would like to take you out again soon," he said.

"It's not your fault and I would love to go out again. I'll check my work schedule and then let you know when I'm off."

Watch me take some vacation time!

"I look forward to it."

Before I could react Kiondre leaned over and placed his lips on mine. I swear on everything I love that I melted into that seat. It had been so long since I had kissed anyone and I had never kissed anyone other than Corey. I mean there was that one time in third grade when Austin Hill was dared to kiss me by his little ugly friends.

I didn't know how long we sat there and kissed but once I saw the light on Ms. Myrtle's porch come on, I jumped like I had just gotten caught. Kiondre burst out laughing causing me to join in and shake my head.

"I better let you go. Be safe beautiful," he told me before he pecked my lips one last time and got out.

My hands were so sweaty and my heart was about to beat out of my chest while I watched him swag over to the steps. Turning around he smiled and waved at me before Ms. Myrtle stuck her head out the door waving at me wildly. I couldn't help but to laugh at her. The lights were off at my mama's house so I knew her and Uncle Cliff were more than likely in bed so I headed home with a smile on my face like never before.

Kiondre

It had been almost three months since coming home and I could finally say that things were starting to look up. Tayler had been able to pull some strings at the hospital where she worked and got me a job as a patient transporter. It may not have paid a whole lot but I was thankful to even be able to work. Every day that I went in I worked my behind off like I was making a six-figure salary just so they could see that I was serious about doing right.

Making my way down to the emergency room I thought back to the night that Tayler and I first went out. I still couldn't figure out who the guy was that I fought but I got the impression that he knew who I was. That was the main reason that I had hauled off and hit him because he was about to air out the dirty laundry that I hadn't told Tayler about. Just the thought of her finding out about my past before I was ready to tell her did something to me and I snapped. The last thing I wanted was for her to judge me or worse, remove herself from my life. We hadn't known one another long but I could already tell that she was special.

Knock. Knock.

Upon hearing the person on the other side grant me access to the room I pushed open the door and walked in. In the bed was a very pregnant woman that looked like she was ready to pop at any second. Her hair was tied up in a scarf with a few of her dreads falling out and framing her vanilla colored skin. No make-up covered her face giving her a youthful appearance.

"Good morning. I'm here to take you down to ultrasound," I told her and she simply nodded.

I unlocked the brakes on the bed she was in before pushing it out into the hallway.

"Where are you taking her?" a man asked from behind me.

Turning around I looked into an older gentleman's face. Something about his simple question sounded off but maybe he was just concerned for his daughter I assumed.

"Oh I'm just taking your daughter down for her ultrasound. You're free to come and wait for her," I offered as politely as I could but the deep scowl that came across his face let me know he wasn't about pleasantries.

I looked down at the patient when I heard her inhale sharply and her eyes were as wide as saucers.

"That's not my father sir he's my fiancé," she spoke up quickly.

"What I tell you about speaking if you're not the one being spoken to?" he said to her sternly while she dropped her head and a tear at the same time.

"I apologize for assuming you were her father but you don't have to speak to her that way," I said.

Now I may have been way out of line but there was no reason for him to go off on her like that when she was just clarifying who he was for me. It wasn't that deep.

"Do you know him?" he asked her still not looking at me. Right then I knew what time it was and I just shook my head.

"No babe I don't."

"I'll show you where the waiting room is," I informed him as I started pushing the bed towards the elevator. I didn't even bother to wait on a response from him. The quicker I could get her downstairs and back, the quicker I could meet Tayler in the cafeteria for lunch.

A smile spread across my face with just the thought of her and I hoped that this patient's test went by fast so that I could get to my girl. The whole elevator ride was quiet as we rode and I texted back and forth with Tay. She was telling me how Nannie kept asking her to come to church on Sunday and I told her to join the club. Since I had come home that was all that she had been asking me but I kept curving her or changing the subject. I knew that she wanted to keep pressing me about it but she knew how sensitive of a subject that was for me so she would drop it for that moment.

It wasn't that I had anything against God because of what I had gone through. Once I got older and was able to really understand Him, I understood that He really did protect me from a life of destruction. When I was younger I didn't see it that way until after I got locked up. I honestly believed that if I hadn't gotten hauled off to jail that I would be dealing with much more than I had been. The enemy had it out for me and it took me a long time to realize it. My reasoning for not wanting to go to church though came strictly from the woman who gave birth to me. It was her demons and the demons of the men of her church that made me not want to be bothered. I trusted God but I didn't trust some of the ones who claimed to be walking in the calling of ministry on His behalf. Those false prophets the bible talked about were real and I wanted no parts of it. If I was going to go to heaven or hell it wouldn't be because I was misled by one of Satan's minions.

The elevator stopped and the doors opened for us to exit. I pushed the gurney out and around the corner to the ultrasound room before stopping momentarily to show the man where he could sit and wait. He made a grunting sound that I didn't even bother to acknowledge before continuing on to the room.

"I'll let the tech know that you're in here," I told her before turning around to leave.

"I'm sorry about my fiancée. He isn't comfortable with me being around other men if he isn't around."

"Understood."

Walking out and closing the door behind me I shook my head at her apology. It amazed me how people couldn't see when they were being abused, myself included. No matter how much I tried to see the good in my mama she never meant me any good and it wasn't until her last visit at the jail that I finally got it. I prayed that the young woman in the room would wake up before it was too late for her. Looking at her chart I saw that she was only twenty-two years old. Her fiancé looked like he was older than me so I already knew the deal with that relationship. It wasn't my business to speak on it to either of them so all I could do was offer prayer on their behalf.

After I let the tech know that they had someone waiting and the room they were in I walked back out into the hallway and answered my ringing phone with my heart fluttering in my chest.

"Hey beautiful," I greeted Tayler.

"Hey handsome."

I could hear the smile in her voice just like I was sure she could hear mine. Never in a million years did I think that I would be capable of having these feelings towards a woman after years of being forced to be with men but this was the best feeling in the world to me. I didn't know if I was in love or not because I had never experienced it but there was a strong possibility that I was. But there was something that was holding me back. All the time that Tayler and I had been spending together alone, with her daughter, and even her mother and uncle I still hadn't explained to her why I was really locked up and what my mother had done to me. Would she think that I was on the down low or be turned off by me even though it wasn't my fault? She didn't seem to be judgmental of anyone but you never knew how someone would act once they were put in a certain situation. That was just something I didn't want to risk. At least not right then. Maybe later on down the road if we decided to take things further I would tell her. Now just wasn't the time.

"I haven't clocked out for lunch yet because I wanted to make sure that you were on the way down here first," I heard her say.

"Give me like ten or fifteen minutes and then I'll be down. I have a patient getting a test done and then I have to bring her back to the ER and I will be on my way. You want to eat here still or go grab something?" I asked. I didn't really care where we went as long as I was with her.

"We can stay here today. I don't feel like dealing with traffic around this time and I know that if I eat and I'm not here I'm going to want to go home and take a nap," she laughed.

"Yeah 'cause you will fall asleep on me in a heartbeat after you eat."

"Awww I'm sorry baby." I knew she was doing that fake pout that I had fallen for. Whenever she did that I was putty in her hands and she knew it.

"Yeah, yeah, yeah. Anyway let me go see if the tech is done so I can hurry up," I told her.

"Ok. See you in a few baby."

Placing my phone back in my pocket I turned and headed back to the ultrasound room just as the tech was coming back out.

"You can take her back now and I'll send these results over to the attending physician. When you get back can you make sure they check the system cause they will sometimes overlook these results," she spoke.

Agreeing to do as I was asked I pulled the bed out and back down the hall. On the way past the waiting room I was a looking for old boy to tell him we were ready but once again he was missing in action.

"I figured he would be gone the moment he had a chance to be," the young lady expressed sadly.

So did I but I didn't bother to tell her. There was no reason in offering my opinion up to her because what would she do? I could tell that he had such a hold on her that she was in way deeper than she even wanted to be. After dropping her off and checking to see if she needed anything I let one of the nurses know to check the computers for the results and headed to see the world's most beautiful woman for lunch.

***

The hour that was spent with Tay just wasn't enough for either of us but we decided to take what we could get whenever we could get it. Just being in her presence gave me so much peace and hope for the future. It was crazy because we hadn't even had sex yet. Not that the thought didn't cross our minds but because of the one thing that I was holding from her was holding me back. Sure we kissed and almost had a slip up but I had stopped it. I could see that she was a little disappointed but I would have been even more disappointed in myself if I didn't give her a choice in the matter. Once I gathered up enough courage to finally open up to her she would be the only one to decide if she wanted to continue seeing me or not. My feelings for her were real and there was nothing in me that had the urge or need for another man.

"I have to stop by and pick the girls up before heading home so when I get there I'll call and let you know unless you want to just come on over," Tayler informed me. We were supposed to be having dinner at her place tonight with Justice and Cadence. Whenever I was with them I felt complete. I knew that neither of the girls were mine but I looked at them in that way so when we were together it was like coming home to my family.

"Let me stop by the house and check on Nannie and change then I 'll be there. That will give you and the girls a chance to get settled."

Leaning down to kiss her soft lips before we went our separate ways we were interrupted.

"I'm pretty sure this kind of public display of affection is frowned upon during working hours," we heard come from behind us.

"Aye man mind your business. I didn't get in yours earlier so stay out of mine now," I told the man from earlier. I didn't know what his problem was but he was about to see a side of me that was unprofessional. Tayler must have felt it coming because she put her hand on my arm as she stepped around me. I thought that she was about to speak to me to try and talk some sense into me but instead she addressed him.

"Corey what I do is no longer any of your business. Now if you don't leave us alone I don't have any problem getting security to escort you out," she told him with fire in her eyes.

"This is Corey?" I asked looking from him to her.

"Mmm hmm," was her simple reply.

"And who are you?" he wanted to know. Buddy crossed his arms like that meant something to me while he stood like he was intimidating the two of us.

Sliding Tayler behind me as I moved up closer I made sure that she was out of harm's way if things went left before I addressed him.

"If she wanted you to know who I was then you would know so I suggest that you just fall back. Unlike you, I know exactly who you are. So move around bruh and head back to your pregnant fiancé."

"Fiancé? Pregnant?" Tayler asked shocked. It wasn't that I was trying to out him in front of her and I hate that I had let that slip out like that. I knew their history, which made me feel even worse about not telling her about my past. She was an open book with me about everything but I let fear of the unknown keep me quiet.

"I'll see you later baby," Tayler got my attention and kissed me on the lips before giving her ex-husband one last hard look.

"Aight beautiful. I love you," I admitted shocking both her and myself causing her to break out in a huge smile.

Neither of us had said those three words to one another since we decided to become a little more serious and I was unsure before if love was what I was feeling. But once I said it I knew in my heart that I was definitely in love with Tayler and it wasn't just because her ex was standing in front of us with smoke coming out of his ears and eyes looking like they were about to pop out of the sockets.

"I love you too Kiondre."

Without another word to Corey or acknowledgement of him still standing there the two of us went in opposite directions. I would be crazy to think that he wouldn't make his presence known again but I would be ready when he did. My mama may have made me wear wigs and sleep with men for money but I was far from being a punk. If Corey wanted these problems that was on him.

Come hell or high water I wasn't about to let anyone ruin my life ever again.

Tayler

Focusing on my work for the rest of the day seemed to be a task that I was failing at. My attention span was that resembling a newborn and my mind couldn't stay on what it was supposed to. Seeing Corey a little while ago caused the anger to rise up in me again. There was a time that I would never let anyone get me out of character and when I did it took a lot to get there. Now days any mention of his name or something that reminded me of him would anger me to no end. And don't let me see his sorry behind because it was worse. It let me know that no matter how many times I said that I was over what Corey had put me through I was starting to see that I hadn't.

I was glad that Kiondre was there with me although I could tell that he was about to go off. The night we went out I saw a side of him that I never wanted to see again and I couldn't let him jeopardize everything that he had been blessed with lately. He had a steady job, a car, and was working towards sawing for his own place. Ms. Myrtle was constantly telling him that he didn't need to move out and he could stay there as long as he wanted but he was adamant about being on his own.

Then there was me.

I had fallen for him so hard and so fast and the last thing I wanted was for him to do something that would cause him to go back to jail. I couldn't take that and I knew that was something that he couldn't take either. From all of the stories that he had told me about his time there I knew that if he went back he may not come out. At least not sane. Even with all that I knew about him I still didn't know the reason why he was arrested in the first place. I had asked once and when he changed the subject without answering me I knew that it was something that he wasn't ready to share with and I was ok with that. There wasn't too much that he could have done that would make me look at him any differently unless he had done something like rape or molesting a child. And trust I checked the registry for sex offenders. Too many women brought men around their children not knowing the type of person he was and then ended up planning funerals or taking their kids to counselors because they cared more about having a man than protecting their babies. Not me though. Justice was my everything and I was going to war with Satan behind her.

Finally the time had come for me to clock out and head home to start cooking dinner. Being that it was Friday evening and I was off for the next two days, I planned on kicking back with my man, daughter, and niece. On the way home I stopped by the store before going to pick the girls up and when I got to Mama's house I couldn't believe what I saw.

"Mama!" I yelled jumping out of the car and running over to her. No matter what funky mood I had been in previously it was gone now while I did my best to stop laughing and help pull my mama and Ms. Gertrude apart.

"Let me go Tayler! I'm tired of her orthopedic knee highs in the summer wearing self. I done told her not to set foot in my house again or I was gonna monkey drag her now get off me!"

Monkey drag? Jesus I'm sorry but that just took me out. I had no choice but to let her go because my arms were too weak from laughing. Mama knew that she was wrong for talking about that lady's shoes when she had some just like it but I wasn't about to tell her and that and make her jump on me. Agnes was old but she was still as strong as an ox. I didn't want those problems.

"Juss come help me," I called out to my child while she was laid out across the steps of the front porch laughing. Oh she was deep in her laughter too because she had tears falling and her mouth was open but no sound was coming out.

"Ahhhhhhh," she finally made a sound before kicking her feet wildly and hitting the wood beside her.

I was on my own.

"Come on Mama the neighbors are looking and Gertrude needs to pull her stockings up. She's flashing everybody," I giggled.

Agnes had literally beat the woman out of her stockings. How she managed to cause the pantyhose to roll down around her ankles was beyond me but that's exactly where they were giving the block a full moon.

"Justice!"

"Ok. Ok here I come," she said breathlessly right before she fell out again and started laughing all over again.

"Jus-," I started as I turned to look in her direction and paused.

This was too much.

Uncle Cliff emerged from the house looking a whole hot mess. It was spring time but the temperature had been close to 90 degrees all week and today felt like the hottest day so far. So I needed someone to explain to me why this man was wearing some velour sweat pants that he had pulled up so far I thought he was gonna strangle himself. His feet were covered in mitch match shoes that looked like they had seen better days, his wife beater was ripped exposing his hairy chest underneath the matching jacket to his pants. That wasn't it though.

Now the last time I saw him, which was this morning, his hair was thick and curly. Why did this man have his hair slick down with a part down the middle and curled up around the edges? He looked like someone had given him a relaxer then took the flat iron and flipped the ends up like we used to wear our hair back in the day.

"Get off of her Agnes!" he yelled from his position on the porch. I already knew that he wasn't about to try and intervene and risk getting hit.

"When I do get off her I'm getting on you next. Looking like James Brown with that hair. All you need is a cape on you back you old fool."

Mama must have finally gotten tired and Ms. Gertrude looked like she was relieved. I give it to her she was trying to hold her own as much as a 70-year-old woman could but Mama was bout that life.

"Ms. Gertrude why do you keep on coming over here knowing Mama asked you not to?" I wanted to know.

"Cause its my man's house just as much as it is hers and if he wants me to come over so I can give him this saved goodness then I will," she sassed while getting up off the ground and bending over to retrieve her stockings. When she did that the wig that was twisted on her head fell clean to the floor.

"Ahhhhhh," Justice screamed out in glee.

"Go get your stuff and get your behind in the car. Ain't nothing funny!" I ordered. She was not making this any easier thinking this was funny. It was indeed funny but I needed to get some kind of resolution so we could leave and I couldn't do it with her being no help at all.

"If he was your man as you call him then you need me to whoop you again for not making him buy you a new wig. Elastic so stretched and you got the nerve to have it sitting up there wobbling like a frisbee. Couldn't be me."

Now she had a point. I don't know the last time I saw Ms. Gertrude with a new wig and from the looks of those struggle braids under it she was due for one.

"Look can we all just calm down please? Uncle Cliff if-," I turned around to my uncle to address him before he suddenly cut me off.

"OG Cliff Daddy! I done told you 'bout calling me anything but," he scolded me.

"You're right. I apologize," I stifled a laugh before continuing. "Uncle Cliff Daddy, I get that this is your house too but why can't you just go to Ms. Gertrude instead of her coming here? You could see each other and then come home to a peaceful house. You got your sister out here acting like she's on an episode of *Love and Hip Hop Senior Edition.* That's not cool."

"I guess we can do that," Ms. Gertrude spoke up.

"You don't have a choice if you want to keep those oversized dentures out the grass," Mama snapped rolling her eyes.

That was when I noticed how Ms. Gertrude' mouth was sunk in like she had bit a lemon and I looked on the ground. Sure enough her top and bottom dentures were strewn about on the lawn.

"Ahhhhh!"

"Get in the car Justice!"

After about another ten minutes or so of calming everyone down Mama went in the house mumbling as I watched OG and his old lady heading off down the street to her house. All I could do was shake my head and get in my car. I knew this wasn't the end of them going at it but I just prayed that sooner or later they would get it together. If not, somebody was going to an old folk's home and I was not playing.

***

An hour later I was finally home and able to start cooking. I called Kiondre and asked him to give me just a little more time before he decided to head over to my house. I needed just a few minutes to myself to shower and handle something that had been bothering me for some time first. So once the food was on and I was comfortable in a t-shirt and some of my old comfortable cotton around the house sweats, I made my way towards Justice's room.

The moment we pulled up to get Cadence my spirit was unsettled for some reason. I may not have been a regular at church like I used to be but I still had a strong prayer life and tried to read my word on the regular. That part had diminished some but not completely. Most people that may have experienced the so called "church hurt" that I had from people who were supposed to be God's chosen, would have completely turned their backs on God. I knew that a lot of people would try to find any reason they could in order justify why God was wasn't real or stay on the path of righteousness but to each his own. I just knew that no matter what my life looked like I would never turn away.

As soon as I got to the bedroom door that was closed I heard what sounded like someone sniffing and muffled voices causing my stomach to drop. I knew that it wasn't Justice crying and that only confirmed my suspicions about something being wrong with Cadence. It had taken her almost fifteen minutes to come out once Jus text her to let her know we were outside waiting. When she didn't respond right away to the text like she normally did I blew the horn and a few minutes later she walked outside quickly. The moment she got in the car she looked like she had been crying. She did her best to act cheerful but I knew it was only a mask that she was putting on. Justice turned around to look at her like she was trying to read her expression but Cadence avoided her glare. I wanted to go right up to that door and ask Sheba what was going on but I knew that it would only lead to us arguing. We weren't too fond of one another for more than one reason but the main one was how I felt she treated the many boyfriends that came in and out better than her own child.

Lightly I tapped on my baby girl's door before walking in to see Justice doing her best to console her best friend.

"What's wrong baby girl?" I asked Cadence as I quickly went over to the two of them.

"I don't know. I knew something wasn't right when she came out of the house and as soon as we got in here she just broke down." The look of concern displayed on Justice was one that I was sure I had as well.

It took almost another twenty minutes to get her to calm down as I held her and Justice watched before Cadence had finally been able to speak.

"Auntie Tay I'm so scared," she got out. Poor thing her voice was shaking just as much as her small body.

"Scared of what Cay?"

"If I tell you please don't say anything to my mama Auntie. I already know what will happen if she finds out someone knows and I don't want that."

Cadence lifted her head with tears falling rapidly and that when I noticed the bruising around her neck.

"Oh my God Cadence what happened to your neck?" I screeched.

"Jayson did it," was all that she told us.

I didn't want to push or force her to go on but I needed to know what was happening inside of that house. I couldn't promise her that I would keep quiet especially if her life was in danger.

"What else did he do?" Justice asked.

Taking a deep breath, she ran down what was going on to us and it took everything in me not to go off.

"Mama lost her job a few months ago and ever since then Jayson has been paying for everything. Including me," she began.

"What do you mean including you?" I questioned.

"He's been staying there since they met but hasn't helped with any of the bills and stuff. So when she lost her job he agreed that he would take care of everything if he could sleep with me. Mama didn't hesitate to let him have his way with me and it crushed me. I begged her not to make me do it and when I did she told me that if I loved her and where we lived that I would do it for our family. She said that she wasn't about to have us put out because I didn't know my place. She's my mama and I love her no matter what but this isn't right. What was I supposed to do? Then when I didn't agree right away she got mad and told me that if I didn't do what he wanted then she was going to put me out. She even told me all of these horrible stories about when she was in foster care and how her foster parents treated her. I can't go there Auntie! I just can't," Cadence cried.

"You know you can come and stay with us," Justice told her but I knew that it wasn't that simple no matter how bad I wanted it to be.

"I can't Jussie. No matter what she's doing I'm scared that if I don't do it for her and I leave he will kill her. It seems like every night he's beating her but she still stays. Then when he's done with her she comes and beats me for making him mad when I didn't even do anything. I know it's because of how she grew up but since she knew what this kind of stuff feels like I thought she would protect me. At least that's what she's supposed to do.

I'm sorry I lied to you about how I got the bruises around my neck a few minutes ago. It wasn't Jayson. It was Mama. She choked me while he did what he wanted with me. Jayson said that he wanted to try something new and wanted her to join in this time. I cried and begged so much until I was tired. He told her that he wanted her to touch me, down there, and right before she had the chance to you beeped the horn and I guess that was God coming to my rescue. I told her that Jussie probably already texted me because you never blew the horn. Mama didn't want to risk y'all coming to the door so she convinced Jayson to let me go so it wouldn't seem suspect. That was the one time that he listened to her."

I was at a loss for words and couldn't stop my own tears from falling. No child deserved for someone to treat them that way especially their own mother. Who raised these people? Cadence was such a good girl and never gave anyone any problems so it hurt me to my heart to know that this was what she had to go through.

"I'm so sorry sis. Mommy isn't there something that we can do?"

"No! You, you can't Auntie. I know he will kill her and maybe me too. Even if you go to the police she will lie for him. I just pray that they leave me alone soon because I swear every time he touches me or she beats me I want to kill them both!"

The look in Cadence's eyes told me that she meant exactly what she said. Her innocence was slowly taking a backburner to the rage that was setting in and I knew that if something wasn't done she would eventually cause some type of harm to either herself or her abusers. Right before I said something to her the doorbell rang. I looked down at my watch and knew that it was probably Kiondre. As much as I wanted to enjoy this evening with him and the girls I knew that Cadence needed me and I was willing to give her that. It was the least I could do considering that Sheba wasn't being the mother she should have been.

"Do you want me to send Kiondre home so we can talk about this some more and figure out what to do later?"

"No Auntie I don't want to ruin dinner. I'll be alright now that I finally got that off my chest. I like when he's around. He's so nice and we all feel like a family. I sometimes wish that he was my dad since I don't know who mine is. Not even his name."

"I have a daddy and I still wish Kiondre was mine. I love how he treats us with respect," Justice agreed shocking me. I never thought to talk to her about what she thought of him but I was glad that I now knew and it was positive.

"Get cleaned up and I'll call you two when dinner is ready."

Standing up I hurried downstairs and opened the door.

"Hey baby," Kiondre greeted me leaning in and kissing my lips before standing up and looking down into my face. "What's wrong? You been crying?"

"It's a long story but I'll be alright," I tried my best to assure him. I didn't know if this would ever be alright.

Closing the door, I went into the kitchen with him following close behind me. The food was almost done and I could feel the tension rising in the air surrounding us.

"It smells good in here," he said. I could tell that the tone of his voice was a questioning one and he wanted an answer to my behavior. As much as I wanted to tell him I knew that it wasn't his issue and there wasn't anything that he could really do.

"Thank you baby. I made some smothered pork chops with onions and gravy, rice, green beans, corn bread, and some banana pudding for desert," I told him.

"Girl if you keep feeding me like this you not gonna be able to get rid of me," he joked. Little did he know I wasn't trying to get rid of him any time soon.

"That doesn't sound like a bad thing to me," I spoke honestly walking over to him.

The smell of whatever cologne he had on made me feel light headed but in a good way as he wrapped his arms around my torso.

"So, you going to tell me what's going on in that pretty little head of yours? I see it all over your face and hear it in your voice."

This was what I was growing to love about Kiondre. He paid attention to everything concerning me and Justice. If we were having a bad day he could tell just by looking at us and he would stop at nothing to make sure that we were alright. If he had to go out and bring her ice cream from Baskin Robins or a simple card that expressed that he was thinking about me, it was the simple things that I adored. Unlike Corey who thought it was always about the money when he bought us gifts and there was no meaning or emotions behind them. Half of the time he didn't even know when I was having a bad day because he was either too wrapped up in work or himself to pay attention to me and our daughter.

"Now I know something is wrong. You just checked out on me and got this faraway look in your eyes. Let me help baby."

My God this man!

"If I tell you something you have to promise me that you won't say or do anything," I told him seriously.

"As long as you or Justice aren't in any kind of danger I promise. Other than that then no I can't give you that."

Yup. He's the one.

"Cadence just told us something that I couldn't fathom happening to a child," I began.

I let him know everything that she had told us and by the time I had finished he had walked off with a look of rage on his face. I knew that he cared about her because she was always around when he was over but I didn't think that it would make him that upset. True enough I was ready to have guns blazing when she revealed her secret but she was like my daughter. I had known her for years and both of the girls had been like sisters since day one. My reaction was understandable but there was something going on with Kiondre that I didn't quite get.

"How is she?" he asked just above a whisper. I heard the crack in his voice so I moved closer to him. The moment I came around and looked at him I saw tears in his eyes that were threatening to fall.

"Kiondre what's wrong?" I wanted to know ignoring his question entirely.

"Hey Kiondre!" Cadence and Justice yelled excitedly. You would think that they were kids catching Santa Clause in the house on Christmas morning.

He turned to them and did his best to compose himself but they picked up on it. It amazed me how much the four of us were so in sync with one another's feelings.

"Are you ok? What's wrong?" Justice wanted to know.

"Cadence are you alright sweetheart?" Kiondre asked causing her shoulders to slump and her head to fall. "Hold your head up Cadence. I don't care what is going on, you hold your head up high. Never let the enemy see that he's breaking you no matter what. That's what he wants and as long as I'm around I won't let that happen. I know I haven't been around long but I look at you just like I do Justice, as my daughter, and there is nothing that I will allow to bring harm to you as long as I know about it. Do you understand?"

"Yes sir," she responded.

"I wished I had someone to protect me back then. Maybe my life would have turned out different," he said more to himself than to any of us. I wondered what he was talking about and I kind of felt that it may have had something to do with his time in jail. We still hadn't talked about what he had gone in for and right when I was about to tell the girls to wash their hands so I could find out the doorbell rang once again.

"Lord who could this be?" I said to no one in particular before reaching the front and opening the door.

"Heyyyyyy Tink!"

Samson.

After the serious situation that had just been revealed I wasn't in a laughing mood but one look at Samson and that was out of the window. I laughed so hard I had to grab my stomach and the look he had on his face not knowing why I was laughing made it even funnier. I don't know what spoke to him when he got dressed but I wish he would stop listening to it.

"What are you doing here crazy?" I finally got the much-needed breath in order to speak.

"Oh, so now that you got a new boo I need an invite to come and see my Tink?" he asked like he was genuinely hurt.

"Of course not I just thought you had gone back home," I let him know while motioning for him to come in so I could close the door behind him.

"I did but I got a job interview in Atlanta the day after tomorrow," he revealed excitedly.

"What? Oh my God you're moving back down south? When?"

"Calm down chica. It's not set in stone yet but I'm hoping so. I miss being close to y'all. I mean I love Chicago and my friends there but nothing is like being here."

"Well I'm glad that you will be close. That will give us plenty of time to hang out and catch up like old times."

"Ummm no it won't," he said popping his lips like he had eaten a lemon.

So dramatic.

"Why not?" I asked.

"Because you got a boo and I need to find me one. I will not be up under you while you are caked up with Mr. Man and I'm lonely. I'm too cute for that," he laughed.

All I could do was shake my head and lead him back to the kitchen area. I had almost forgotten about Kiondre being there until he started coughing uncontrollably on the drink that he was placing back on the table. It took everything in me to stifle the laugh that was threatening to erupt. We all knew how Samson got dressed in the dark but if you were meeting him for the first time, the ash on his exposed skin and colorful ensemble could startle you.

"Hey Sammy!" the girls called out running to him.

"Pause. What your eyes doing all puffy?" Samson asked Cadence. He too could pick up on when something was wrong with any of us no matter what it was. I knew this wasn't the time to tell him because he would set it off and none of us wanted that right now.

"They were just laughing when I told them about Mama and Ms. Gertrude getting into a fight and her teeth fell out," I covered for them.

"Bout time! I thought Auntie would never lay hands on that old hag. She couldn't wait for my mama to gone on to glory before she sunk her withered fingers into my daddy," Samson said sucking his teeth.

Did I mention that Samson was Uncle Cliff's son? My bad.

"She needs to be worried about that rhema arthritis that she got and leave him alone," he continued on in his rant.

"Rhema arthritis?" I asked out loud.

Before I could ask Samson what in the world he was talking about Cadence, Justice, and Kiondre were howling in laughter.

"Ahhhhh," screamed Justice falling around on the floor while Samson and I looked on lost until it hit me too.

"Fool! You mean *rheumatoid* arthritis?"

That was it. All of the anger and sadness that I had been previously feeling was momentarily put on the back burner as I joined in on the laughter. There was no way that I could be around Samson and not get a good laugh. Maybe that was his gift, to lift people's spirits.

"What's funny?" he wanted to know. He was seriously confused.

It took us a few minutes to get under control and when we did I decided to finally introduce my cousin to Kiondre.

"Cuz this is my boyfriend Kiondre and baby this is my cousin Samson," I introduced the two of them.

"Nice to meet you," Kiondre stood up to shake his hand.

"Ok then Tink you did real good for yourself. He's nice on the eyes and has manners. As long as you treat my boo right young man you will be alright with me. I hate to have to lay hands like it's Communion Sunday again but for this one right here I'll go to war," Samson informed him pointing one of his press on nails in my direction. I had no clue why he still wore those things but you couldn't tell him to let them go.

"Well that you don't have to worry about. As long as she lets me I'll do my best to keep her happy," Kiondre expressed. The look in his eyes when he looked at me let me know that he meant every word that he was saying and I couldn't help but to blush.

"Ewwwowww," Samson made a noise that resembled a cat in heat. I guess that was his *'I'm excited'* noise because he was grinning and dancing around like someone hit him with a taser.

We all made small talk while I made the plates and the girls set the table. I was glad to see that Kiondre wasn't uncomfortable around Samson. Some straight men seemed to be on edge when they came in contact with homosexual men and I never understood it. We may not agree with their lifestyle but they are still human and deserve respect. Whatever God felt about what they did was between them and Him. Samson's choice was his and his alone although sometimes I wondered if he was truly happy or if he had just gotten comfortable.

I grabbed the food and headed to the table before saying grace. Just as we were about to dig in the doorbell rang yet again.

"We not gonna ever get to eat," I thought as I went to answer it. If I had known what was waiting on the other side of it I would have just ignored them. Now here I was face to face with Satan yet again.

I stood emotionless and unresponsive as I looked at Corey standing there with a smug look on his face. After seeing him at the hospital earlier I knew that he was going to show his face eventually, I just didn't know that it would be this soon. But we were talking about Corey and he loved to rub salt on open wounds. I would never forget the day that I was released from the hospital and came home to find his sanctified mistress and her husband waiting in our living room. They could pretend all they wanted that she was there as a spiritual leader checking on her flock but I knew better. Corey was being his inconsiderate and petty self by rubbing her in my face and I paid neither of them any mind.

"What are you doing here?" I asked not really interested in his answer.

"I can't come see my wife and daughter?" he asked smugly.

"Cut the crap. We both know you're not here because of me or Justice so what do you want?"

My patience was running thin with Corey and if he kept pushing me he was going to get a side that he had never witnessed before. Or maybe I could just yell for Samson to handle it while I watched. Instead of answering me right away Corey focused his attention to something behind me causing me to look myself. If I wasn't so mad I would have laughed at the sight of Samson holding my brand-new frying pan with his lips poked out. Following closely behind him were the girls and lastly Kiondre.

"Why don't you ask your man there why I'm here?" Corey nodded his head in Kiondre's direction.

"How about we ask this frying pan how it feels against your forehead," Samson snapped.

"Or we can ask *him* the reason that he was really in jail."

Suddenly my heart dropped into my stomach when Corey mentioned Kiondre being in jail. I should have known that he would go around snooping once he found out about my new relationship but to know that he knew something that I didn't, didn't sit well with me. I don't know what it was but I had a feeling that things were about to change.

Kiondre

Two weeks after what was supposed to be a dinner with my new family I was still holed up in my room. I hadn't been to work, my cell was turned off, and all I heard was Nannie constantly walking around the house praying day in and day out.

Tayler's ex-husband had exposed the one thing that I had yet to reveal to her. The way he made it sound was like I was on the downlow and that if she didn't leave me alone he would make sure that she never saw their daughter again. I had fallen so deep in love with both her and Justice that I didn't even force her to make a decision and just left. What hurt the most was that she didn't even come after me but I understood her position. As a mother, she had to do what she had to do to protect her. It would have been selfish of me to ask her to do anything that forced her hand.

Knock. Knock.

Instead of yelling to tell Nannie to go away I stood up and went over to my bedroom door and opened it to see her weary face. I knew that she wanted to console me but I didn't know how to let her in to do so. At one point I had even gotten mad at her because I felt like she should have fought to take me away from the daily hell I went through. Then again during that time she had been really sick. The moment she was better though she did try to take me but the courts made it hard. She was on a fixed income and couldn't give them a valid reason as to why they should. Being that she didn't want to risk me being placed in the system for telling the truth she decided to try to come up with another plan. Right when she thought she had something to help me I ended up going to jail for second degree murder.

"Nannie I don't feel like talking right now," I told her as respectfully as I could without her being offended.

"I understand baby but I think it's time for you to get this off your chest. Release it once and for all and tell Tayler exactly what happened."

I knew that she was right but I wasn't trying to place the woman that I loved in an uncomfortable spot. She probably didn't even want to be bothered with me anymore anyway. I waited a whole day to see if she would call or text but when she didn't I just turned my phone completely off. If she had tried to reach me and I didn't answer, she never made any efforts to stop by. So I took it as us being over before we could ever really get started.

"I'm sure she doesn't want to hear anything that I have to say."

"She's in the living room so hurry up." With that she walked away.

My emotions were all mixed up knowing that she was here. On the one hand, I was excited to see her. I just wanted to hold her in my arms and never let her go. Then on the other I didn't know if she was there to curse me out and tell me that she was disgusted with me. Taking a deep breath I wiped the sweat beads forming on my head and went into the living room. The moment I rounded the corner Justice ran right to me wrapping her arms around my waist.

"I missed you so much," she whispered.

Hugging her back I told her that I had missed her but I never took my eyes off her mother. Tayler knew that I meant what I had said was directed to the both of them. Seeing her sitting there I could tell that she was just as stressed as I was but she was in a battle of her own. Instead of going to her like I wanted I just gave her a weary smile which she returned with one of her own. Even though she was sad I was just happy to see her.

"Baby it's time for you to explain everything," Nannie let me know. "And sweetie please hear him out before you say anything. I know that the way you probably got the information had you thinking one way but please hear him out."

Simply nodding her head, Tayler agreed. I peeled Justice from my body and instructed her to sit beside her mother. Any other time I wouldn't have had this conversation around her but since she was already aware I felt that she needed an explanation too. I just hoped they understood.

"First, let me apologize for not telling you this sooner. I never said anything in the beginning because I never saw me falling in love with you baby. Once the feelings started to surface I knew that I should have said something but I was afraid that what we had would end. Never did I intend on hurting you and the way that you received it wasn't how it really is."

I stopped talking to get myself together while trying to gage how she was feeling about what I had told her so far. Instead of accepting my apology right away she just waited for me to continue. I took a deep breath and put it all out on the table.

It was Sunday morning and mama had just gotten me dressed for church. She told me that I was gonna be the sharpest five-year-old little man in God's house that morning. I had on my white suit with a sky-blue tie and a fresh pair of white dress shoes. Mama said I looked just like my daddy but when she said it there wasn't a smile on her face. I didn't understand why.

After she finished getting dressed she grabbed my hand and we walked the few blocks down to Mt. Olive Baptist Church. Mama didn't have a car and I heard that she blamed daddy for not having one just like I heard her blame him for other stuff.

Once we got into the church it was filled with people lifting up their hands and praising this God that no one could see. There was this lady that was hopping up and down in the middle of the aisle causing her shoe to come off. I snickered and Mama grabbed my arm tighter shaking it and giving me that look she gave me all the time. The one that let me know that she was about to backhand me if I didn't act like I had some sense.

Moving closer to the front I noticed a man looking at me with a look that I couldn't explain. He didn't look mad but he didn't look happy either. I tried my best to hide behind my mama's leg so that he couldn't see me but she quickly pushed me to the side. Had it not been for the wooden bench I'm sure I would have hit the floor and messed up my suit. That would have really made her mad and I could only imagine the whipping that she would give me when we got home.

The whole time the pastor spoke about sins and redemption the man in the front kept looking at me. A few times he smiled and once he looked at Mama and nodded his head causing her to hold her head up higher than she was before. I didn't know why I was feeling scared all of a sudden but then I understood once everybody started to leave.

I paused giving myself time to think about if I wanted to go any further with my past but I knew that in order for Tayler to fully understand my position I needed to tell her everything. No matter how hard it was or what she would think afterwards. I had held back enough of my past and maybe, just maybe, this would be what really set me free.

"Take your time," Tayler spoke softly. Her voice and the calming tone that it carried instantly eased my nerves. I knew that she was anxious but I could tell she didn't want to push me to the point where I closed up again.

"There were only a few people hanging around after church was over," I continued. "Mama spoke to them with this big smile on her face and hugged each of them. I wondered how she knew these people and if that was the same church that Nannie went to so I asked.

"Mama is this Nannie's church too?"

"No baby Nannie goes somewhere else. This is our church," Mama informed me.

"But why can't we go to her church?" I asked but instantly got scared with the look she had on her face.

"Sister Laura! It's so good to see you in service today," the creepy man said but he was looking down at me. "And who is this handsome young man?"

"Oh this is my little prince Kiondre," she told him.

"It's nice to meet you Kiondre."

"Boy where are your manners?" Mama asked. I was so scared to answer her that I felt like I was about to pee in my

clothes. Just the thought of that happening made me open my mouth quickly. She was already going to be mad about my manners and I didn't want to add to it.

"Nice to meet you too," I almost whispered.

"Deacon Johnson I have that information about the upcoming Vacation Bible School that you asked for," she let him know.

"Oh good. Well let me make sure that everyone is gone and the front is locked because we will be in the back office. You can go ahead and head down there and I will join you shortly," Deacon Johnson instructed.

Mama hurriedly rushed us down the back hallway and with each step that I tried to keep up with I felt like I couldn't breathe. I wanted to cry but I didn't know why. We waited for a few minutes before the creepy man, or Deacon Johnson as she called him, came into the small room. The suit jacket he wore was off and he threw it on the chair that sat against the brown book shelf.

"Is everyone gone?" Mama asked.

"Yup and I made sure to lock up," he replied.

"Good. Now where's my money? Mama wanted to know with her hand outstretched.

"You sure he's ready?"

"I'm sure you know how to get him ready."

Reaching into his pants pocket he pulled out a stack of money, counted some bills off, and passed them to her. Quickly *flipping through the money Mama looked up at him with her face twisted up.*

"What the hell is this? We agreed on a thousand Eugene not five hundred!" Mama yelled.

"Once I'm done I'll give you the rest. I have to make sure I get the full hour that you promised me. How do I know that you won't take my money then interrupt me before my time is over?"

"Whatever. One. Hour," my mama told him while I sat and watched in confusion as she walked to the door and opened it. Not bothering to say one word to me before she left.

Deacon Johnson came over to me and I could feel the tears pooling up in my eyes. Something was wrong and I wanted to go to Nannie's house. Her house was the only place that I felt completely safe.

"Why the tears?" I heard.

I ignored him and did my best to pray to the God that Nannie always spoke so highly of. She said that He was everywhere but I didn't feel like he was nowhere in that building. I had to pray to Him so that he could show up and save me. But He didn't.

Before I knew it, my small frail body was standing naked in the middle of the floor as Deacon Johnson unhooked his belt buckle and let his pants fall to the floor. I was so full of fear that I stood frozen and cried silently.

"God Nannie said you would help me. Where are you?" I asked silently. Nannie said that I wouldn't see Him but to always

know that He was there. I couldn't. I needed to see God so I would feel safe.

"I want to go home," I cried hoping that Deacon Johnson would understand and let me go.

"You will son. As soon as we are done. You want to play a little game?" he spoke in a hushed tone.

I shook my head no while tears flew down my face.

"Yes you do. Your mama told me you would like this game."

I knew that was a lie because Mama never played any game with me so she couldn't possibly know what I liked to play. He was lying and I knew it. I didn't care anything about my clothes as I tried to back up and run out of the door but it was locked. And I moved too slow.

Grabbing me from behind, I tried to scream and fight but there was no use. He covered my mouth so that my screams were unheard. I cried harder than I ever had in my short life. That was until the pain hit me and I became numb. Instantly the tears dried up and I stopped fighting. I couldn't move if I wanted to. I remember feeling that man's heavy body over mine as he moved back and forth but that was all that I remembered.

After that day, the woman that was raising me had allowed her demons to change me. They changed me into a different person each and every time her beloved church members wanted to have their way with me. Or when she would find other people that she knew who had a thing for children.

When I turned thirteen she told me I was grown and now I needed to dress the part. Since when were thirteen-year old's considered adults? I had just stopped wetting the bed only a few months prior and now I had to dress like a girl. Long wigs, tight clothes, make-up; she even made me wear women's undergarments. Mama would even teach me the mannerisms of a woman so when I went to school I got bullied on the regular. I got suspended so much for fighting that I eventually dropped out. Every time I had to sleep with a man I started to harden my heart a little more and hate my mother more than I had ever hated anyone in my life. Even the men that took advantage of me.

For as long as I could remember Mama had never brought a man around that she was interested until one day she introduced me to Amir. She told me that he was her boyfriend and that they were serious. I could tell that she was in love with him by the way she looked at him but I didn't see the feelings being reciprocated. Instead the lust in his eyes was directed towards me.

Amir started off just coming around when she was there and some part of me knew why he would come to the house when he knew she wasn't there. We didn't have sex for a while until one day I thought I had fallen for him. My mind was so messed up that I didn't understand what I was going through. I had even tried sleeping with this girl I met once to make me feel normal. That didn't last long though since I was confused.

Anyway, my mama was supposed to be going out of town the following week when something hit me. The love she was showing Amir made me angry. How could she love someone else more than she loved me? I was her child but she continued to treat me like a dog. So now it was my turn. I flirted hard with Amir whenever he was around, even when she was there. I would walk

around the house in revealing clothes that still hid the fact that I
was a boy and I could see him eating it up until one day I
suggested we take it further.

My plan was perfect. The moment she left I was on the
phone letting Amir know that I was ready to go there with him.
Before I could get out everything I wanted to do with him he was
knocking on our back door. It was all fun and games until he
started kissing on me and trying to get my clothes off. Up until that
point he still had no idea that I wasn't a girl.

When we got into my room he told me that he had to go to
the bathroom so I used that time to quickly undress and get under
the covers.

"Oh my God it's now or never," I thought as I watched
Amir emerging from the bathroom and getting undressed.

I had been with plenty men before now but just like always
I was shaking like a leaf. Pulling the covers up under my neck
something in me told me that this wasn't right. I had such a bad
feeling and I tried thinking of a way out of it but I knew that it was
too late. I had fallen for Amir, or at least I thought I had before
that very moment. This was the time that I needed for my revenge
but was it really worth it? Should I let God handle the punishment
my mama so rightfully deserved or do I do it on my own? I once
heard Nannie saying how people would step in to hurt the people
that hurt them thinking that it was justified instead of letting God
handle it. Causing Him to deal with us for over stepping our
boundaries. He doesn't need our help we need his but our flesh
gets in the way.

"What's good? You changing your mind on me?" Amir
asked me.

"No. It's just that this is my first time and I'm a little nervous," I lied through my teeth.

"Don't even trip. I'll take my time I promise."

Deciding not to say anything I just smiled at him as he moved closer to where I sat. The moment his knee hit the bed and he went to pull the covers back we heard the front door open.

"KiKi!" I heard my mother yell.

"Shoot!" Amir said in a panic while I sat frozen in place.

This couldn't be happening. Not now. My mama was supposed to be out of town for the weekend at a church retreat and here I was sneaking around with her boyfriend.

"You just gonna sit there?" Amir asked as he fumbled around with his pants.
Before he could get his left leg inside of his jeans my door burst open and there stood my mother.

"What is going on here?" My mama asked as soon as the bedroom door swung open. Stopping dead in her tracks she just stood there with her mouth wide open in shock and tears forming in her eyes.

As bad as I wanted to roll my eyes at my mother I didn't. Did I want her to find out like this? Did I want her to hurt like I was hurting? Of course. I just wanted to succeed in my plan first before I ended her world. Well that was my intention.

"Baby it's not what you think," Amir did his best to explain reaching for her.

"Oh, it's exactly what I'm thinking! You're about to sleep with my son!" She yelled and I dropped my head.

"Son?!"

"Yes, my son Kiondre," my mama shrieked before she snatched my wig off.

If looks could kill I would be dead. And if the looks from both my mother and Amir didn't kill me I was sure that the bullets from the gun he was now holding would do the job.

"This the kind of stuff y'all do huh?" Amir asked. He was seething with anger as I   on scared out of my mind.

Neither of us were able to speak and that must have infuriated him even more. The sound of the safety being removed from the gun let me know that I had to act fast. I remembered taking the gun that my mama had stashed away in her closet about three weeks before. It was the day that I was going to end my own life. I was so tired of what I was going through and even though I believed that if I killed myself I would surely go to hell, it had to be better than living here. The only thing I couldn't figure out was how to take off its safety. When I did I heard Nannie come in the house and call my name causing me to panic and throw it under my pillow.

Reaching slowly as Amir paced the room looking back and forth between Mama and me I was able to grab a hold to it.

"Man, got me up here bout to sleep with a man yo! I ain't no faggot!" he screamed.

"Baby just calm down," Mama tried her best to sweet talk him.

"Nah! Ain't no calming down. My wife gonna kill me."

"Wife?!"

If that didn't knock the wind out of the both of us I didn't know what could. Had there not been a gun in my face I probably would have had something to slick to say but there was no time for that.

Pow!

The shot rang out as the three of us watched the blood leaking from Amir's exposed chest. He reached his hand up to touch the hole that was there with a scowl on his face. Amir staggered backwards while Mama stood there crying before she tried to reach out to him. It took every bit of strength for him to raise the gun again, this time in her direction.

Pow! Pow!

Amir's body hit the floor and Mama's screams filled the entire house right before I heard the sirens getting closer. I knew that after the first shot one of the neighbors would call the police and I wasn't surprised that they were fast. The neighborhood that we lived in was one that was respected thanks to my body being sold to afford it.

"Drop your weapon!" and officer yelled out.

Doing as I was told, seconds later I was tackled on the bed with my hand behind my back. Once they tried pulling me up and noticed that I was completely naked they covered my lower body with the sheet and had my mama help put some shorts on. The whole time she did, her glare was cold. Colder than I had ever seen and for the life of me I couldn't understand it. Not once did she try to console me or ask how I was.

"Ma'am what happened here?" another deputy asked pulling out a notebook as they pulled me away from the room. The EMT had just arrived and they were trying hectically to revive Amir. I heard one say that his pule was faint but he had one.

"My...my son shot my boyfriend."

"I shot him because he had a gun pointed at the two of us and he was about to shoot my mama," I cried.

Noticing the confused looks on the two black men's faces one of them went back to the room only to return a short period later.

"The only gun in there was the one that you had," he told me holding up the gun that was now inside of the evidence bag.

"That can't be. He just had it in his right hand when I..." I began but trailed off realizing what was happening.

"There was no other gun. I came back home because I left something for my church retreat to find my son about to have sex with my boyfriend. They had never met before today so he didn't know that Kiondre likes to dress as women and trick men into sex for money. I'm surprised no one else had killed him before today for pulling this stunt," Mama stood before me and lied like it was nothing.

"Mama!" I cried out.

"Sir we couldn't help him. Time of death 1:36 pm," an EMT came out and told us.

As soon as the officer that had been holding me the entire time started reading me my rights I watched a sly smile come across Mama's face. Instead of me hurting her she turned around and hurt me more than she ever had. I couldn't believe that I was about to go to jail for protecting her. Maybe I should have shot her instead.

Tayler

When Corey told me that he had information on why Kiondre had been in jail I knew it was serious but I wasn't prepared for what he had to say. Hearing that he killed the man that he was trying to seduce was a lot but to hear that he was living on the downlow was too much. For some reason though I didn't believe the last part. I was just about to tell him to get out of my house so that I could find out what was going on but his threat about taking Justice from me shut me up. The way that Kiondre looked at me I knew that he wasn't going to make me choose him or my child and for that I was thankful.

I cried like a baby for the rest of the night and even called in to work the next day. When I finally did pull myself from under the covers I tried calling his phone but it went straight to voicemail. I knew that he was hurting and I wanted so bad to go to him but I felt like my hands were tied. I knew that Corey would make our lives ten times harder and I couldn't have that. If it

hadn't been for me having connections in the hospital I would have never known that Kiondre hadn't been to work but luckily, I was quick with a response. I informed them that he had a family emergency but he would be returning as soon as he could. Stacy was cool so she wasn't pressing the issue. By him never calling in and going above and beyond every day, she decided to use some of his PTO for the days that he was out and once he ran out she said that she would just say that he was excused. If Stacy hadn't been almost sixty years old she would have gotten the side eye 'because I thought she had a thing for my man.

Now sitting here listening to Kiondre tell me the truth my heart broke even more. I should have stopped him from leaving and let him explain but I didn't. Once again, I let Corey dictate what I did and it could cost me the happiness that I had finally found. Not only that I had to hear Samson's big mouth go off on me the moment Kiondre pulled off.

"Baby Tink and Little Mama go upstairs right quick while I talk to your mama and deadbeat…I mean daddy," Samson instructed the girls. Without any hesitation, they ran up to Justice's room and shut the door. The moment we heard it click I knew that it was about to be some problems and Corey should have taken that opportunity himself to run. Now normally I would try and stop Samson from going off but this time it was justified. At least to me it was.

Whap! Whap! Pop! Whap!

The way Samson flew around me and started raining blows on Corey was like nothing I had ever seen before. I've seen Samson in quite a few fights but that fight was by far the worst one.

Whap!

Corey hit Samson so hard his head snapped back and I could see blood flowing from his nose.

"Samson!" I yelled and went towards him but stopped dead in my tracks. I wanted to kick myself for not having my phone on me because we were definitely going to need some law enforcement backup. I thought about calling for Justice but I didn't want her to witness her father get laid out like a rug.

Samson didn't lose his footing behind that hit Corey delivered which surprised me. As hard as it was he should have been on the ground but there he stood motionless. Watching the scene unfold on my front lawn was like watching a car crash. You didn't want to look but you couldn't turn away. The way Samson brought his head back up and turned to face Corey in slow motion, I knew that he was about to kill that man.

"Nigga you still hit like a little girl!" Samson laughed before he took off on Corey again.

I had to do something because if I didn't Samson was going to be hauled off to jail for a lengthy sentence and I couldn't have that.

"Come on cousin that's enough. You did enough damage!"

"Nah, he wants to come around here threatening you just because you moved on and I'm not having it. He gone learn today," Samson said just as serious as a heart attack.

"Samson the police are on the way," I told him once I noticed the sirens were getting closer. Corey was sprawled out on the lawn like he was on a beach somewhere sun bathing and I couldn't help but to giggle.

When I turned back around I almost peed in my clothes from laughing at what I saw. Samson had pulled the wig off that he was previously wearing off and placed it on the ground beside him and was flapping around like a fish out of water. All I could do was shake my head and wait as the three police cars pulled up and the officers got out and rushed over to me with guns drawn.

"Ma'am are you alright?" one of them asked me. I could see their faces had questioning and confused expressions plastered across them so I decided to explain.

"Yes, I'm fine. My ex-husband showed up here uninvited and when I asked for him to leave he threatened me. My cousin then asked him nicely to go away so my husband hauled off and hit him in the nose and Samson defended himself," I halfway told the truth. I could hear my mama's voice telling me that a half truth was a whole lie but I pushed that to the back of my mind. I would repent as soon as this was all over but there was no way that I was about to tell them that Samson attacked first. If Corey wanted to come over with his mess then he was going to take this loss, or 'L' as the young kids said, and deal with the police.

"What happened to your cat?" another officer asked.

"Cat?" I asked confused. When I saw him point down at Samson's wig on the ground I lost it!

I don't know how long it took me to stop laughing before I could let them know that wasn't a cat on the grass but a wig. When I did they couldn't help but to join in.

"Does she…I mean he…do they need medical attention?" the first officer asked me. Bless his heart he was so confused as to how he should address Samson and his red face told me just that.

"No, he will be fine but my ex just might."

Thirty minutes after the fight ended and all statements were taken, Corey tucked his tail between his legs and declined any medical assistance before leaving. Samson's dramatic self on the other hand was still laying on the grass peeking through one eye.

The moment he saw someone look in his direction that nut hurried up and closed his eyes and played possum.

"What am I gonna do with you? Get up and let's go in the house crazy," I giggled nudging him with my foot.

"Girl the po po gone?" he asked me.

"Yes chile."

"Oh, good cause you know I can't go down to the jail. I'm too pretty for that and don't have time to be slaying heads in the penitentiary."

"Samson what?" I wanted to know.

"Now Tink you know if I go to jail everybody in the alternative lifestyle section gonna see how good I look and want me to do their hair and give beauty tips," he explained.

"Boy bye! You know you are the only one that thinks you are a fashionista. Trust they won't bother you for not one tip or hair do."

"Was that shade?"

"No boo, that was a whole forest," I replied.

When we walked back in the house the realization of Kiondre being gone kicked in again and I couldn't help but cry. Samson sat on the sofa beside me and just held me close.

"Tink you need to go to him," was all that he said.

"I can't."

"Sit up," he instructed and I did what he asked. "Let me tell you something. The man that I have been hearing about for months and the one that I met today loves you. I can see it in his eyes. That old saying 'the eyes are the doors to the heart...'"

"The eyes are the windows to the soul," I corrected him shaking my head.

"Yeah that's what I meant. Now hush so I can be real deep. Anyway, like I was saying, the eyes are the windows to the soul and they tell me that whatever Corey implied was not true. If it's one thing I know it's men and he is not a down low one. I live this life that I do by choice but there are others out there that live it because they were forced to and feel like there is no way out. You need to hear him out before you lose one of the best men you have ever had. Corey may be dumb but he ain't stupid. He knows he don't care nothing about Baby Tink because if he did he would do right by her no matter if y'all are together or not. He's just doing this because he can tell that you have moved on and not worried about him or those little elf ears his ugly daddy gave him."

"Samson."

"What? We all know it's true. Take you a breather and then go to Kiondre. If what he says is something that you really can't deal with then let him know why. But if it's worth it fight for him."

Everything that Samson told me I understood but still didn't act on it. I cried day in and day out whenever I thought about Kiondre yet I didn't call or go by. That was until Ms. Myrtle called me and told me the state of mind that he was in. She begged me to come over and just hear him out. I knew that he needed me just like I needed him so here I was. Crying yet one more time but for a different reason.

"I'm so sorry baby. I should have let you explain what happened," I said softly.

Pulling me into his strong arms, which I had started to call home, I could feel the rapid beat of his heart. It matched my own.

"Shhh. I don't blame you for your reaction. I should have been honest in the beginning so that you would never have to be put in that kind of situation. I would never make you choose between me or Jus. That would be selfish of me to even ask. Where do we go from here?" he asked me nervously.

I thought a for a few minutes and couldn't think of anything else to do. I only had once choice.

"We pick up where we left off."

The smile that he gave me let me know that he was relieved and in agreement with me. When Justice ran over and jumped on the two of us I couldn't help but to laugh. Leaning over he kissed me and this time it felt different. All of the kisses that we shared previously were intense but I could tell that now that he had released his burden he could give himself to me fully. Because of that I was now willing to give him my all no matter what Corey tried to do.

Kiondre

Neither of us paid any attention to Nannie when she got up and walked out of the room until after I finished telling Tayler and Justice my secret. I was so glad to have my woman back in my life that I didn't care about anything else at the moment. Only thing was that no matter how happy I was there was part of me that was beginning to feel like I was about to deal with something else. When she came back she was holding a small envelope in her hands.

"I'm so glad that the two of you had this talk and worked things out. Y'all are gonna need each other when I finish," Nannie told us. I could tell that she was nervous by how she played with the corner of the envelope. Justice got down off of our laps and sat beside Tayler. The whole atmosphere had changed and I was concerned.

"Nannie what's wrong?" Tayler asked the same question that I was scared to get the answer to.

"About a year and a half after you were locked up and young girl just randomly walked up to me in the grocery store. Well at least I thought it was random. She knew who I was but I had no clue as to how. She started to tell me how she had been wanting to come and talk to me but she was scared and after she saw you on the news about what happened she decided against it. When she saw me come into the store she knew that it was a sign."

"What did she want?" Tayler asked.

"She said that she wanted me to meet my great granddaughter."

"Wait what? Great granddaughter? How is that possible? I'm my mother's only child and I don't have any kids," I expressed to her confused out of my mind.

"She said that it only happened once and some months later she found out that she was pregnant. Considering that she hadn't slept with anyone else she knew that the baby was yours," Nannie explained some more.

"Come on Nannie. You watch enough of these paternity court shows to know that women be lying about stuff like this. For crying out loud I was sleeping with men," I went into a rant and then stopped. Just that fast it hit me like a ton of bricks. The one and only time that I had sex with a female could I have possibly fathered a child?

"Trust me baby I thought about that but then she reached in her purse and handed me some pictures of the child and asked me if I could give them to you. Before I could respond she ran out of there like her hind parts were on fire."

"What was her name? Why did you tell me before now?" I inquired. I could feel my chest beginning to tighten and my anger rising. Tayler must have noticed it too because she placed her hand on my back and began to rub it soothingly.

"I didn't even get a chance to get her name Kiondre and I didn't tell you because of everything that you were going through. I didn't want to add to it especially if it wasn't true. You were just seventeen years old and in jail for killing somebody. The life you had up until that point wasn't at all the best. How could you have handled something like that?"

"She's right Kiondre. That would have been too much for you to have to face."

This was why I couldn't risk losing Tayler. When I was off track she was there to help me think rationally. Nannie was right. There was no way that I could have fathomed being a father when I didn't even know how to be a man. During that point of my life I was confused.

"Do you still have the pictures?" Justice asked. I had forgotten she was still there.

Nodding her head, Nannie opened the envelope and pulled out what looked like three pictures before handing them over to me. Water fought against my eye lids as I looked at the pretty little caramel toddler looking back at me. Her sandy brown hair was done neatly with those colorful ball things and barrettes at the end and her face was lit up like a Christmas tree. She looked so happy and I was good knowing that if she was my child that she was well taken care of.

"Oh my God," whispered both Tayler and Justice at the same time.

"What's wrong?" I'm sure my furrowed brows let her know I was confused.

"I know her," Tayler told me with tears of her own escaping her now closed eyes.

"How do you know her?"

"I know her because that's Cadence."

Tayler

Just when I thought my life couldn't get even more complicated there was another monkey wrench thrown into the mix. How in the world was it possible that Cadence was Kiondre's daughter?

"Are you sure?" Kiondre asked me looking about as dumfounded as I felt.

"Does the little girl in that picture have a beauty mark beside her lip and her left eye?"

I watched as he studied the pictures. Yeah so?"

Reaching into my pocket I pulled out my phone and went to the most recent picture of Cadence and passed it to him. As soon as he compared both of the pictures he sat back like the wind had been knocked out of him. Nannie snatched the phone and held her free hand to her chest.

"How did I not know this? I see this baby and Justice all the time and not once did I think that this was the same child."

"Don't blame yourself Nannie. It's not like you could really tell. Her hair color is different and she's older now," Kiondre told her. "This explains why the day we went to pick Cadence up from her house and I was in the car I thought she looked familiar. I didn't think anything of it but now I know it's because she has my eyes. I was looking right into my own. What am I gonna do?" he asked no one in particular.

"You're gonna sit down with her so you can let her know and then do everything in order to get her away from that house."

Looking up at me I saw worry in his eyes but I was dead serious. I had a feeling what was going through his mind. What if Cadence resented him or was ashamed of his past? What if him coming into her life now caused more harm than good.

"Listen baby. I know that you're probably worried about how she will handle this information but I honestly think she's do just fine. The relationship that you have built with her is new but it's strong. How you responded to her situation showed her that you really do care about her wellbeing."

"What situation?" Nannie wanted to know.

Kiondre took the time to explain to her what we knew and while he talked all she could do was cry.

"Oh my Lord. God no...not again," she wailed. I knew that she was in emotional pain and I could only imagine her feeling like history was repeating itself.

Watching her break down I rushed to sit beside her and wrap her in my arms. I didn't know what God had in store for us but I did know that Kiondre didn't go through what he did for nothing. As painful as it was I knew there was a lesson in that trial. True enough I didn't understand why God would put us through situations that could break us then turn around and use that very thing to mend us right back together. Kiondre and Cadence had gone through their break and now it was time for their mending process to begin. This time as father and daughter.

"I need to get this over with. Do you mind going to get her for me and bringing her back? I can't go another day knowing this

and not doing anything about it no matter what happens she needs to know."

"Not at all. Want to ride with me?" I asked him. I knew that if he sat here in his thoughts he might allow himself to slip back into his hole and I didn't want that. I just prayed that if he agreed to go that the pickup would run smooth. Especially us knowing what was going on behind those walls.

"Um yeah. I can't just sit here or I'll drive myself insane. Or talk myself out of this," he told me causing me to smile. It made me feel good to know that we were in sync to the point where we knew each other's thoughts and feelings. It showed me that we truly paid attention to one another and were growing together.

Fifteen minutes later we were pulling into Cadence's yard. I told Justice to text her before we left just to make sure she was ready.

"Did she respond?" I asked Justice looking at her in the rearview mirror.

When she looked up into my face I already knew the answer and my heart started beating fast. Kiondre picked up on it and reached for the door handle before I could stop him and jumped out. Taking my seat belt off as fast as I could I jumped out with Justice right behind me.

"Help!" Cadence screamed and Kiondre lost it.

The sounds of him beating on the door sounded like thunder roaring in the sky because he was hitting it so hard.

"Cadence!" Justice called out.

"Watch out," Kiondre instructed pushing us back some.

Taking a few steps back he lunged at the door before it came flying off the hinges. It took everything in my power not to dwell on that moment because God knows it wasn't the time. But Jesus on the mainline that man was fine!

The screams coming from the back of the house brought me back to my senses and the three of us rushed towards them. I wished we had just waited for him to come back because the scene that was before me would forever be embedded in my head. Not only my head but my daughter's.

"What the hell is going on here?" Kiondre yelled.

Sheba had lost her mind! Cadence was a child and to see her strapped to the bed while her mother did things to her that made me sick to my stomach while her no good boyfriend stood there recording them and pleasuring himself. Jumping into action Kiondre went off on Jayson and I gave Sheba a beating that she would never forget.

"You sick, trifling, no good heffa! Abusing your baby for some damn money all for a no-good nigga! You're supposed to protect her and make sure that nobody gets close enough to hurt her but here you are trading her body for some chump change!"

"What was I supposed to do?" Sheba wailed.

Instantly I stopped beating her and twisted my face up so much I'm sure it looked like I was going through an exorcism. Did this ditzy broad just ask what she was supposed to do?

"What were you supposed to do? How about get up off your behind and find another job and not one that involves pimping out your fifteen-year-old daughter!" I was tired of talking to her just that fast so I resumed her beat down until I felt arms wrapping around me and pulling me away.

"Let me go! Let me go!" I screamed. I was not done with Sheba and if whoever was holding me didn't let me go they were about to catch these hands too. That was until I heard the static of a radio.

The police. If I got arrested for this I was going to do my time with my head held high. Sheba getting beat up was worth it if I was able to help Cadence. But Lord knows I was tired of seeing the police. I imagined what I was feeling was equal to repeat offenders when they kept getting locked up for doing dumb stuff. The only difference was that I hadn't actually gotten arrested any of those other times. But I was sure that my luck had rung out. If so this last kick was gonna be worth it I thought as I took my right foot and kicked her as hard as I could.

"Hey! That's enough! I don't want to arrest you because I know the reason this happened but if you don't comply with what I'm asking you to do then I will have no choice but to take you down town for resisting."

Hearing him tell me that gathered me so quick and I stopped trying to be the next Laila Ali. I watched one of the women officers as she handcuffed a hysterical Sheba.

"My baby! Where is my baby?" she screamed.

"You mean the one that you were just in here raping? She's with her father!" I shouted back.

Now listen, I know that wasn't how things were supposed to come out but the way her eyes got big was priceless.

"That's right Kiondre is her father and he knows now. You better believe that he's gonna do everything that he can to make sure she is taken care of. I knew that it was a reason I never liked your little bald headed self. What kind of mother are you?" I was furious and I didn't care how she felt about it either.

She didn't even have the balls to say anything which was most definitely the best thing for her at the moment. If she knew like I knew she would tread lightly. I may have stopped fighting her but if she popped off at the mouth I was just going to take one for the team.

The officer that was escorting Sheba sucked her teeth in disgust while walking out of the room. I could only imagine what would happen once Sheba got booked and the other inmates found out what she was in for. She was gonna get what was coming to her and I can't say that I was sad about it. Cadence suffered and so would her mother and Jayson. All I could do was shake my head before the officer let me go and I went in search of Kiondre, Justice, and Cadence. It was about to be a trying time for them but I was going to be there every step of the way.

Kiondre

Sitting in the living room with Cadence cradled in my arms felt surreal. I didn't know how to be a father or what I was supposed to be doing so I just held on to her as tight as I could and let her know that no one would ever hurt her again. Tayler spilled the bean in the room and I wondered if Cadence had heard her. If she did she hadn't opened her mouth to me about it just yet and I wondered what was going through her mind.

We sat on the sofa and watched as the police pulled both Jayson and Sheba from the back room and they both looked horrible. Sheba's left eye was swollen shut and her hair looked like there were only patches left. My girl had really done a number on her and I shook my head slightly. The way Sheba looked made me nervous for anyone else if they were to ever come at Justice. Cadence wasn't even Tayler's daughter and she had beat that woman silly, I could only imagine how bad it would be if she was protecting her own child. If Corey didn't know how she got down he might want to back off with the threats. The beating I gave him wouldn't even compare to what Tayler was capable of. I made a mental note to never make her mad.

Jayson was another story. When I walked into that room and saw baby girl screaming and crying I instantly got sick to my stomach. All I saw was red noticing that he was pleasing himself to that sick mess and I lost it. I beat him so bad I knew that he was going to need some type of surgery to correct his face and maybe even some physical therapy. That's if he made it. The way the officers were looking at him with just as much anger as I felt, I was sure that they wouldn't let him get away without a few blows of their own. I completely understood the way people felt about police and the brutality they issued out on innocent people, I even agreed with them. But it was times like this where I wouldn't utter a word about which life mattered the most because how I saw it, the only life that mattered was my child's. If Jayson or Sheba turned up on the 6 o'clock news because they didn't make it to the police station I wouldn't type one hashtag or raise one black fist in memory of them.

I was so deep into my thoughts I didn't hear when one of the officers or Tayler said something to me.

"Huh?" I asked coming out of my daze.

"Baby Officer Reynolds needs to talk to us," Tayler spoke again.

Nodding my head, I tried removing my arm from around Cadence so that I could go and talk to the two of them alone but she wouldn't let me. Her small arms compared to mine held on for dear life and when I looked down into her eyes they were pleading with me not to go.

"We can talk right here that's fine. I understand the circumstances are quite difficult and I want you all to be as comfortable as possible right now which I know may be a little hard," she told us before sitting down on the love seat across from us.

Tayler went and sat on the other side of Justice and pulled her close. Just like Cadence, Justice was a nervous wreck. I could only imagine how she felt seeing her best friend who was more like her sister going through this. They were going to have a long road to recovery but unlike me, they had a solid support system.

"Cadence, I know you may not want to talk too much about this. If anything, I'm sure you want to forget it as quickly as possible but I need to ask you some questions," Officer Reynolds spoke kindly.

"It's ok," Cadence replied just above a whisper.

"How long has this been happening?" she asked pulling out a pen and note pad.

"Since my mama lost her job a few months back," Cadence began explaining. By the time she was done telling her story for what I'm sure felt like the millionth time, Officer Reynolds looked like she wanted to cry herself.

"Wow. I'm so sorry you had to endure all of that Cadence. I've heard so many stories like this since being on the force and just when I thought that I've heard the worse the next one always seems to top that one," she sighed. "We are still going to need you to go to the hospital so that a rape kit can be done on you. The recording that we gathered on Mr. Jamison's phone is already in our possession and that is more than enough to have them both convicted. The two of you won't have to worry about any charges being brought against you for assault because you were protecting Cadence. I'll make sure of that."

"Thank you so much," I told her. I was glad to hear that our freedom wasn't on the line because I couldn't risk being away again.

"Excuse me?" an older white woman got our attention.

There were so many police and detectives going in and out gathering evidence like it was a murder scene that we didn't notice her come in.

"Can I help you?" Tayler asked her.

"I'm looking for Cadence Hamilton."

"And you are?"

Once again Tayler was in protective Mama Bear Mode and all she was concerned about was protecting Cadence.

"My name is Lois Dickerson and I'm a social worker from the Department of Family and Children Services. I received a call about a minor being assaulted by her mother and that I needed to come and remove the child from the home. We need to place her somewhere until we can find either another family member or an adequate foster home."

"No! I don't want to go with you!" Cadence screamed before bursting out in tears again.

"Sweetie I understand how you must be feeling but-."

"Tuh! You know how I feel? Did your mama sell your body for Birkin bags and rent money? Or maybe you mean she beat you then put her mouth on areas of your body that she wasn't supposed to."

Cadence's rant caused everyone in the room to stop what they were doing and look at her. She had gone from being scared, to hurt, to angry and if she was anything like me, the anger taking over wouldn't be good for anyone.

"I-I-well no that's not what I meant. I just sympathize with you," Ms. Dickerson tried to backpedal. You would think that as long as she had been in her position she would be used to handling these kinds of things but Cadence's response looked to have thrown her for a loop.

"If you sympathize with me then just leave me alone and let me go with my daddy," responded.

All of the air in the room felt like it had been sucked out and I didn't know how to respond. I was sure that she wasn't in the room when Tayler told Sheba so was she talking about me or someone else? I had just found out that she was possibly mine and to think of her talking about another man being her father began to crush me until she spoke again.

"Daddy can I go with you please?" Cadence looked at me waiting for an answer.

She heard?

"Yea baby girl. Of course you can," I assured her as I kissed her forehead.

"And sir what's your name?" Old lady Dickerson asked. For some reason, she was getting under my skin and I already knew that she was going to be a problem for us.

"Daddy," Cadence snapped sassily. If we weren't dealing with such a serious situation I would have laughed at the face she made. It resembled mine so much when I got mad. Lord I was a father with a daughter. What in the world was I going to do.

"My name is Kiondre Andrews," I finally revealed.

I watched her pull out her mini iPad and begin typing away before her demeanor changed drastically and I knew what time it was. Cadence was about to be taken away from me and I had just gotten her.

"Mr. Andrews I'm afraid that Cadence has to come with me."

"And why is that?" Tayler asked.

"It looks like Mr. Andrews was convicted of murder and we have to think about the safety of the child," she explained.

"Whatever you were just looking at it should also show you why he was in jail and that he was released for good behavior. If he can't take her then I will. But you better believe that she won't be leaving out of here with anyone other than us." Tayler's attitude and patience were both on a hundred and steady rising.

"Ms. Dickerson, is it?" Officer Reynolds interjected. She probably knew that if she didn't, Sheba and Jayson weren't the only two that would be going downtown.

"Yes."

"Can I speak with you outside for a moment please?"

Instead of giving a verbal reply Ms. Dickerson moved towards the door followed by Officer Reynolds. Everyone sat in silence waiting on the two of them to return. I took that opportunity to silently pray to God.

"Lord I know that just like most I don't talk to you as much as I should. There's even been times that I questioned if you would even hear from me if I did. For all of those times I apologize and

ask for your forgiveness. I say that I trust you but I don't always show it.

God I'm asking that you please hear me this time. Don't let them take Cadence from me and put her somewhere where she will continue to be abused. I know that I don't know the first thing about being a father but you do. You're the best father that anyone could have and I ask that you guide me on this journey. Give me a chance to do something great and use my past to help her.

For years I asked why did you allow me to go through so much pain from the age of five until recently, now I know. No one else can fully understand what Cadence is dealing with but I can. Allow us to use this as a way for the both of us to get healing from. She needs me just as much as I need her father. Please lay it on Ms. Dickerson's heart to leave her with me. Whatever I have to do to make this work God I'm willing. Have your way in this Lord. In your son Jesus' name I pray, Amen."

My heart felt like it was going to burst in my chest as I cried like a baby and held on to Cadence. I didn't know if this would be the last time that I saw her and I needed the both of to remember this hug forever just in case.

"Kiondre."

I looked up at Tayler looking like she was about to break at any moment and that's when I noticed both Officer Reynolds and Ms. Dickerson standing beside her with somber looks of their own and I knew. They were taking Cadence and there was nothing that I could do about it. I felt defeated once again in life but I guess it was just God's will and I could do nothing but accept it.

Epilogue

"Amazing God, Amazing king, amazing everything

Amazing God, Amazing king, you're an amazing, amazing everything
Amazing God, Amazing king, amazing God of everything
Amazing God, Amazing king, he's an amazing everything

With All the mistakes that I made. My life would be controlled by fear.
Lord if I didn't have you near. By now I would have lost my mind, I would have lost my mind.
God I wouldn't have no peace, no peace, no peace. But I'm so glad that I've found you."

I sat watching *Young Worshippers* praise dance to William Murphy's *Amazing God* and the words hit home. Visions of my past came flooding back to my mind and I couldn't help but to be overwhelmed. The pastor had just finished a sermon about going back to your past and getting stuck in it after God told you to leave it where it was. He explained that looking behind you at what used to be could cause you to be stuck like Lot's wife. She had instructions along with the rest of her family to leave Sodom and not to look back on what was behind them because those consequences would be everlasting. Instead of listening to Him she turned around anyway. Her disobedience caused her to be turned into a pillar of salt.

The visions of my past while each word played weren't because I was going back to them though. It was because I was remembering where God brought me from and being appreciative of those bad times.

Walking into Deacon Johnson's office.

Where would I be without you. I would probably be in a grave.

My young body being taken advantage of.

With All the mistakes that I made.

Killing Amir.

My life would be controlled by fear.

The beatings I received in jail.

Lord if I didn't have you near.

Mama's abuse and the blame for my father leaving.

By now I would have lost my mind, I would have lost my mind. God I wouldn't have no peace, no peace, no peace.

Receiving a second chance at life by being released from jail, falling in love with Tayler, and a chance at being a father to Cadence.

But I'm so glad that I've found you.

Amazing God, Amazing King, amazing everything.

Standing to my feet I couldn't help but to raise my hands in the air and praise The Lord. No matter what my circumstances looked like I realized that God was always right there with me. Keeping me sane. Keeping me covered. In spite of what was going on with me, He was growing me. For that He deserved all the praise I could give.

"You rule throughout the land, you give life and breath to every man. You sit high and look down low, earth is your footstool, heavens your throne," I sang along with the music.

Watching my daughter dance her heart out I knew that she may have been feeling the same emotions that I was. Her face no longer showed the sadness we all saw for months after her ordeal. Now it showed strength and determination of not letting it control her.

When Officer Reynolds and Ms. Dickerson came back into the house the day we found Cadence being assaulted I just knew that they were going to take her from me. I guess the prayer that I had prayed reached God's ears and in return He touched Ms. Dickerson's heart. They were acting like they were about to deliver some bad news that I didn't want to hear when in actuality they were trying to hold back tears of their own.

Again, God had showed just how much he planned out our lives even before we were formed in our mother's wombs. Officer Reynolds or Chelsea as she was called by her peers in school, had been one of the few people that was actually nice to me when I was there. All of these years she said that she had prayed for me and didn't know why. Every night she asked God to make sure that I didn't hurt anymore. When she saw that I had been arrested for murder she prayed even harder. She even had her parents and church members lifting my name up.

While she talked Tayler had a strange look on her face but once she found out that Chelsea was happily married and her husband was even praying her attitude changed.

My little jealous thug.

If it wasn't for Chelsea explaining to Ms. Dickerson everything and how she had no doubt that I would be the best person to take Cadence I would have lost her that day. Now here I was watching my little big girl lifting up the name of The Lord right beside my step-daughter and her sister. Looking to my left and locking eyes with my wife, she gave me a warm smile and squeezed my left hand that was now at my side.

Besides God and Nannie, Tayler had been my angel sent straight from heaven. Never once did she judge me on what I had gone through and even after she found out the gritty details she stayed. Her love was declared each day by not only words but her actions. Most women would have high tailed it in the other direction when they heard that I had been intimate with men no matter if it was by choice or by force but not her. Never once did she treat me like I was some kind of freak or on the downlow. Her love was real just as much as mine was. Because of that I knew that I couldn't let her go so I married her and here she was looking as beautiful as ever carrying our first son.

Tayler was a rare breed. Had it not been for her I never would have forgiven my mother. Tayler expressed to me how important it was for me to do so. Not necessarily for her but for myself. I never knew why she was so tormented by the demons in her life that had ended up changing me but it wasn't for me to fix. I just needed to forgive her, let her know that I loved her, and then let God do the rest. I prayed that before she took her last breath a month ago that she had finally asked for her own forgiveness and entered in the arms of God. That was something that I would never know.

The day I poured out my heart to her in the hospital she let me know then that she was still the same mean and unapologetic woman she had always been. But when I walked out of that room that day my burdens were no longer my own and the chains of bondage had been broken. I never returned to see her the whole time she was there and after a while Nannie stopped telling me about when she would go visit. It wasn't that I didn't care about what happened to her but she made it clear that she never wanted to see my face again and I was fine with that. Maybe she would find peace and we would reunite in heaven.

After church was over Chelsea and her husband Terry who was the pastor at the church invited us to dinner but we had to decline. Mama Agnes wanted us to all come over for the longest but our schedules were hectic. That day was the only one that we finally had free and we had promised her.

I was glad that we had been able to find another church home because I knew we needed it. As the head of my family I had to be in my rightful place and make sure that my family was being fed and led in the right direction. If I was out of line I now knew that nothing else would go right and with everything going wrong before I couldn't chance that.

"Y'all ready?" I asked my girls.

"Yes cause Mama cooked me some pig feet like I asked her too and I can't wait to get to that pot," Tayler told me excitedly.

"Ewww," both girls squealed.

"More for me," Tayler replied shrugging her shoulders nonchalantly and wobbling out the door.

I was glad to see my wife and daughter so happy these days. They too had had some trying times with her ex-husband Corey. He tried everything that he could to wreak havoc on our lives once he found out that Tayler and I were still together. When he couldn't stop the process of me getting Cadence legally he went as far as to represent both Sheba and Jayson in their cases. All of his attempts failed and just like his clients he was now having to do a long sentence of his own. So much stuff came out about his legal practices and other criminal activities he was involved in that he was disbarred and thrown in jail. God definitely worked in mysterious ways. But we were now free to live our lives free of the three of them. I had even been able to adopt Justice since Corey had no problem signing over his rights as a father. It wasn't like he was one anyway. Tayler was worried that his decision would hurt Justice but it was actually the opposite. I had never seen her so excited since I've known her and it made my heart swell with joy. Now all of us shared the same last name and I couldn't be any happier.

Pulling up to Tayler's mother's house we saw her cousin Samson getting out of his car at the same time. I swear I think he was color blind or maybe just blind altogether by some of the getups he was constantly in. The only time I saw him dressed somewhat normal was when he went to work and even then it was a stretch. And bro never saw a lotion bottle in his life! The outfit of choice that he was wearing this time made him look like he was a rejected member of that dance group the girls loved watching on Lifetime. The Dancing Dolls or something like that.

Samson had on a yellow catsuit with brown fringes down each side. It looked like something that he had made himself because the way it was sewn crooked and with gaps in between let me know that a professional couldn't have done that. On his feet were some clear jellies with little kitten heels on the back and they were about three sizes too small.

Jesus his head.

I was starting to believe that PETA needed to be called cause something had to give. We could not keep seeing him with forest animals strewn about his head covered in arts and crafts paint. Whoever the hair stylist was that kept contributing to the destruction of those poor bears and rabbits needed her license revoked.

"Heyyyyy family! Ohhh look at y'all looking all blessed and highly savored."

"It's favored Sammy," Cadence said laughing and giving him hug.

"Yeah that's what I meant," he said before hugging the rest of them and giving me a pound.

Walking into the house the smell of Agnes' southern cooking instantly hit my nostrils making my stomach growl in anticipation.

"Well look who decided to show up," Uncle Cliff laughed.

"Don't do us like that OG Cliff Daddy," I told him patting him on the shoulder. I learned real quick that if I didn't call him by the name that he suggested those old hands of his still worked. He punched me one time in my arm so hard I almost forgot he was elderly and Taylor's uncle and was about to go toe to toe with him. Ever since then he was address just like he wanted.

"Old man leave people alone," Samson told his daddy.

"If you stop taking your eye balls out before getting dressed looking like a ghetto kaleidoscope I will," he snapped back.

"Ahhhhhh," Justice screamed in laughter. I had become so used to hearing her laugh like that when she was beyond tickled that it caused me to join in with her.

"Stop all that fussing and lets eat before this pregnant woman in my kitchen eats it all," Mama Agnes told us.

"They shole better cause me and KJ getting' it in! Mama where's the hot sauce and vinegar?" Tayler asked coming into the room with a bowl of pig feet licking her fingers.

"Don't tell her Mama. I'm not about to be up all night with her popping Tums and complaining cause she has heartburn and my baby won't be still," I told her.

"That's why I hid it before y'all got here."

Just as we were all going into the dining room to the table the doorbell rang and both Uncle Cliff and Mama Agnes almost broke their necks trying to get to it first.

"I know good and well you not coming to my house again Gertrude," I heard Mama Agnes fuss.

"Agnes it's for good reason this time. I need to talk to Cliff about a little situation," she explained nervously.

"What could possibly be that important that you are risking me snatching yo' teeth out cho' head again?"

"I'm pregnant!" Gertrude yelled. Tayler almost needed the Heimlich done the way she started choking at that revelation.

I couldn't lie, I was stuck like whoever Chuck was too.

"Pregnant? How is it possible to get pregnant with powdered eggs? Lady if you don't gone on somewhere!" Samson jumped in.

"Ahhhh!"

"Hush Justice!" everyone yelled at her but it didn't matter. By then she was on the floor in a fit of giggles.

I was wondering though myself how Gertrude had gotten pregnant. I knew that it was possible but God couldn't have that big of a sense of humor.

"Gertrude I done told you whatever gas bubbles you feeling ain't no baby and if it was it's not mine. After this one right here," Uncle Cliff paused to point at Samson. "started dressing like a Skittles factory I put my soldiers out the army. Couldn't chance that happening again."

"Daddy! That's cold," Samson faked like he was hurt.

"Not as cold as you are. Look at them little knocking knees you got."

That time I couldn't help but to hold my stomach and let out a hearty laugh. These people were a riot but they were also my family. Once Gertrude left and Nannie showed up we could all finally sit down and eat. I sat back and looked at all of the people around me and could only silently thank God for it all. I had a closer relationship with him, a good stable career, a beautiful wife and daughters, and from the looks of it I was about to welcome my son into the world.

Tayler's water had just broken.

The End

Special thanks to my classmate Brie "BrieTheAmazon" Dixon...I told you I wouldn't forget you! #Muah

CPSIA information can be obtained
at www.ICGtesting.com
Printed in the USA
LVHW02s0122191217
560223LV00040B/2017/P